An Eerie E-mail

There was an e-mail from Brad, but Traci skipped over it as if he had never existed. Pop-Tart forgotten, she began clicking on the new messages, growing more astounded with each one.

They all said the same exact thing.

CAN YOU COME OVER TODAY?

How many times had Corky called and asked her that very question? Probably as many times as she had called and asked *him* to come over. Hundreds. Thousands.

It was insane. Crazy. Freaky.

Hysterical.

And that was exactly how she felt: hysterical. She was talking to a ghost. But how? And *why*? Why was Corky getting in touch with her *now*, just as she was starting a new relationship with Brad?

A Girl, A Guy & A Ghost

Sherrie Rose

smooch

New York City

SMOOCH®

October 2003

Published by

Dorchester Publishing Co., Inc.
200 Madison Avenue
New York, NY 10016

ISBN: 0-8439-5276-8

Printed in the United States of America.

Visit us on the Web at www.smoochya.com.

To my niece, Traci Lynn Jones.
Having you in my life has brought me great joy, and I
thank God every night for blessing me with the opportu-
nity to watch you grow from a sweet, fat-cheeked baby to
a beautiful, warm, loving wife and mother.
I'm so very proud of you!

A Girl, A Guy & A Ghost

Chapter One

"So, are you going to invite Brad to your mom's annual Halloween party?"

Cradling the Cricket phone against her ear, Traci Nettleton considered her best friend's question as she flopped onto her back on the bed and stared at the glow-in-the-dark stars pasted to her ceiling. They were pretty sweet when the lights were out.

Almost as "sweet" as Brad Davidson.

"Trace?" Christine Abernathy prompted when she didn't answer. "Are you? Don't tell me you're going to chicken out!"

"It's not that. It's Mom. You know how weird she can get—especially on Halloween. I don't want her to embarrass me in front of Brad." She loved her mom, she really did, but she wished she'd act more like other moms instead of one of her teenage friends. Most of her friends, including Christine, envied Traci for having a "cool" mom. Traci didn't think they'd feel that way if *her* mom were actually *their* mom.

"I think your mom's cool."

Traci suppressed a groan. Christine was *so* predictable! "Yeah, well, I'd trade places with you in a heartbeat."

"Would not."

"Would too!"

"Would not! You'd have to give up your cell phone, your Internet, and share the bathroom with my two little brothers. And don't change the subject. You're going to invite Brad, and that's that."

"Bossy."

"Chicken."

"Grow up!" Before Christine could retaliate, the bell announcing a new e-mail dinged from Traci's computer speakers. "Hang on; I've got a message. I'm gonna check it out." She muttered a silent prayer that it was from Brad. He'd e-mailed her twice, and both times he'd hinted that he was interested in getting together with her. She was hoping he'd come right out and ask her. Her friends were pushing her to ask *him*, but Traci preferred to let Brad do the asking.

She rolled from the bed and walked to her computer, peering at the screen. Holding her breath, she clicked on Read Messages. A message popped up on the screen: *GREETINGS, BOBCAT!*

She nearly dropped the phone. "Oh . . . my . . . God, Christine!"

"What? What is it?" Christine's voice sounded shrill with frustration. "I hate it when you do that to me! Who's it from? What does it say?"

Voice shaking, Traci read out loud to Christine. "'Greetings, Bobcat.'"

"*Bobcat?*" Christine echoed. "What the heck does that mean?"

Traci's heart was pounding so hard she could see it fluttering against the oversize T-shirt she wore as a nightgown. Her mouth had gone dry, too, and she wondered if this was what it felt like before a person fainted or had a heart attack. "Christine, if you sent this, it's not funny!"

"Did you forget? I'm grounded from the Net for two weeks because I forgot to pick up my bratty brother from softball practice. Besides, I don't know what you're *talking* about, and if you don't tell me I'm going to start screaming in your ear!"

"He . . . the only person who's ever called me that is dead!"

Christine didn't speak for a moment. Finally she said, "You're talking about Corky? That cute little boy who lived down the street from you? Your first boyfriend?"

Traci swallowed hard and nodded, then realized Christine couldn't see her. "Him," she croaked. "Corky Evans. He . . . was my best friend before he became my boyfriend."

"Traci, you never told me that he called you boobcat—"

"*Bob*cat," Traci corrected faintly.

"Whatever. You and I didn't become friends until after he . . . he drowned, didn't he?"

"Yes." Traci felt hot tears spring to her eyes. There wasn't a day that went by that she didn't think about him. They had been inseparable. In fact, they had spent the night with each other on weekends until they were eleven, when his mother caught them

12

playing doctor and nurse and decided it was time to keep a better eye on them.

Swiping at her eyes, Traci said, "He called me Bobcat because he said I had pointed little ears like a bobcat."

"Man, Traci, you're weirding me out. Are you sure about the message?"

"I'm staring at it now. It . . . it even says it's from the Undertaker. That . . . that was the nickname he used on-line. The Undertaker was his favorite wrestler."

"I'm sure a lot of people use that name," Christine pointed out.

"Maybe." Traci bit her lip. The tears continued to fall. "But I don't think this is a coincidence. The message says 'Greetings, Bobcat' and it's from the Undertaker. If it's a coincidence, it needs to be on *Ripley's Believe It or Not.*"

"I hear you. Ooh, girlfriend, you're making my skin crawl."

"How do you think *I* feel?" Traci asked, unable to take her eyes from the screen. "I'm standing here staring at it."

"Send a reply."

"What?"

"Send a reply! Ask him who he is. That's the only way you're going to find out, because we know that message didn't come from a dead person, right? Call me back if you get a reply."

"No!" Traci shouted. "Don't go! Stay on the phone.

I'm scared." This time she wasn't ashamed to be chicken. She suspected that Christine was scared, too.

"All right, but hurry. Mom lets me talk on the phone until ten, remember? After that she pulls the plug. Stupid brats. You're so lucky you're an only child...."

Traci tuned Christine out as she sat in her computer chair and typed a brief message and clicked the Send button. She could hear her heart beating as she waited, and the drone of Christine's voice in her ear as she launched into a tirade about her pesky little brothers and how miserable they were making her life. Traci wasn't rude enough to tell her friend that she'd heard it all before, but she was thinking it.

The message went into cyberspace. Traci closed her eyes, trying to imagine the message humming along the cable cord to another server, then another and another until it popped up God knew where.

She kept her eyes closed until the bell dinged, scaring her so badly she nearly wet her pants. Wouldn't *that* be embarrassing!

"Whoever he is, he's quick," Christine said, apparently hearing the announcing bell. "Hurry and read it. I'm dying here. Oops. Sorry. No pun intended."

The words tried to run together as Traci stared hard at the message screen. No way. No friggin' way. It was impossible! She took a deep breath and read out loud, "It says, 'I'm the boy you could never outrun. You're the girl with a birthmark on her butt.'"

14

"How the heck would he know that?" Christine asked in a squeaky, fearful voice.

"He . . . he tried to paint me nude once. His dad walked in on us. We got an hour-long lecture I don't think I'll ever forget."

"How old were you guys?"

Traci felt her lips tugging at the memory. "Eight, I think. The painting turned out lousy, but we had fun."

"Sounds like it." She paused a heartbeat. "Traci? What's going on? We both know this has to be a hoax. Maybe his brother or sister—"

"No siblings."

"What about his mother—"

"She would never, ever do that to me." Traci was absolutely positive about that. In fact, the last time Traci visited Mrs. Evans, the poor woman told her that she had yet to touch anything in Corky's room.

"Man, this is too weird," Christine said.

Cradling the phone against her ear again, Traci typed in another message, asking his name. It *had* to be a hoax—she knew that—but she couldn't resist finding out just how cruel the person on the other end could be. This time the sound of Christine's voice gave her comfort as she waited for a reply.

The bell dinged about a moment later, giving Traci the impression he or she had been waiting for her to ask the question.

"Winston Evans," she whispered, her eyes going wide.

"What? What did you say, Trace?"

She cleared her throat and said it louder. "Winston Evans."

"Well, there you have it. Must be a cousin or something. Whoever he is, tell him from me that he's a creep."

"No." She quickly typed in another message and sent it. "Christine, Corky's *real* name was Winston. Not very many people knew that. He hated it."

"Well," Christine said dryly, "obviously *someone* else knew. Oh, come on! Surely you're not falling for this hoax?"

Traci ignored her, her burning eyes on the screen. She had just asked him to tell her something nobody else could possibly know. If the person knew Corky at all, then he would know that she and Corky had plenty of secrets, secrets that she was positive Corky took to his grave.

In a shadowy corner of Corky's basement where they had operated on "deceased" animals, they'd made a blood pact. They'd made that pact the day Mrs. Ryder's cat got ran over by the garbage truck. She and Corky had tried to put the poor thing back together, although they both believed the cat to be dead. In the middle of the "operation," the cat's eyes had popped open. He'd let out a horrible screeching noise before racing out the basement window, trailing a sewing needle and thread behind him.

Nobody had ever seen the cat again.

Another message popped up. Traci clicked on it, feeling as if she'd stumbled into a bad dream. There in bold capital letters—something else that was exclusively Corky—was the message, *DO YOU STILL HAVE THE RING YOU STOLE FROM BISHOP'S DRUGSTORE WHEN YOU WERE TWELVE? AND DO YOU STILL KEEP IT IN THAT LITTLE WOODEN JEWELRY BOX I MADE FOR YOU ON YOUR THIRTEENTH BIRTHDAY?*

Traci gasped and covered her mouth. Corky and Corky alone had known about the guilt she'd suffered, how close she had come to taking it back and confessing to Al Bishop. But fear and embarrassment had stopped her. She'd ended up keeping the ring as a reminder that she wasn't cut out to be a shoplifter.

Corky had sworn a solemn oath that he would never tell a soul.

"Traci, what's going on? Why are you so quiet?"

"I'm . . . I think I'm going to puke or faint or something," she said.

"I think you're supposed to put your head between your knees," Christine said.

If she did that, Traci was certain she'd fall right on her head. "Give me a minute," she whispered. She read the message over and over, and in the end it still said the same thing. On trembling legs, she got up and walked to her vanity table and opened the ugly

17

wooden jewelry box Corky had made with his own two hands.

There it was, as she had known it would be.

The cheap ring she had stolen from Bishop's drugstore. Even if Corky had told someone about her stealing the ring, they couldn't have known where she kept it, because not even *Corky* had known.

Chapter Two

Traci turned off her computer without going through the proper channels of closing Windows. For good measure, she crawled beneath her desk and yanked the power cord from the wall outlet.

Then she scurried out and stood, backing away, swallowing hard, staring at the computer much the same way she had stared at Mrs. Ryder's poor cat when it came back from the dead.

For the first time in more years than she could count, Traci wanted to cry for her mother. It was only the third time she could even remember having such an impulse. The first time she'd screamed for her mother she'd been stung by a wasp. The second time she'd *wanted* to scream for her was the day they had resurrected Mrs. Ryder's cat.

Traci nearly jumped out of her skin when Christine spoke into the phone.

"Are you okay, Trace? Do you want me to come over?"

"You—" Traci's voice came out hoarse and croaky. She tried again. "You're grounded, remember?"

"This is an emergency. I think even *my* mother would understand."

Understand, maybe. But not believe them. Who would? Certainly not Traci's beautiful and bubbly mother, Susan. Her mother believed in horoscopes and love at first sight and was convinced that pink went with red, but she would never believe that

Corky was talking to Traci through the computer.

Traci made a tiny sound, clutching her throat, still staring at the blank screen. Of *course* her mother wouldn't believe it, because it wasn't true.

It was a hoax. It *had* to be a hoax.

"Traci? Did you by chance fall and hit your head?"

Now, *that* she hadn't considered. She did now. And nope, she couldn't remember anything remotely connected with a head injury, much to her great disappointment. "No, I didn't," she whispered into the phone.

"Why are you whispering?"

"I don't know."

"If it's a ghost, he can probably hear us whispering. He can probably hear us thinking, too."

Christine was just too cheerful to be believed. "There is no ghost." So why *was* she whispering?

"Okay."

"Don't patronize me."

"Wouldn't think of it."

Traci took a deep breath and two more steps away from the computer. The backs of her knees hit the bed. She slowly sank onto it instead of flopping in her usual way. "I turned off the computer."

"Good thinking," Christine said, her voice slightly louder than Traci's. "If we did drugs, we could blame it on hallucinations."

"But we don't do drugs."

21

"Why would we?" Christine parried. "Our lives are interesting enough without them."

"You got that right." Ghosts coming back to tease her . . .

"Remember that movie, *Ghost in the Machine*?"

"Shut up." This time Traci meant it. She was freaking out enough without Christine tempting her imagination.

"Are you going to tell your mom?"

"No."

"Oh."

Traci frowned at the phone, then put it back to her ear. With her free hand, she took a strand of her blond hair and began twisting it around and around. "You think I should?"

"I don't know, but if it were me, I'd get out of that room."

"But it's *my* room." Traci realized what she was doing to her hair and made a disgusted face, dropping her arm. She'd broken that habit years ago, after her aunt Gillian told her it was causing her hair to break.

"But what if *he's* listening?" Christine asked.

"There *is* no 'he,'" Traci whispered as she raced for the door. She jerked it open and ran to the hall landing before she forced herself to slow her panicky pace. Downstairs, she could hear her mother singing in an off-key voice as she revamped her nails. Susan did her nails every single night before going to bed. It wasn't the only beauty ritual she performed; Traci knew that her mother would also have a mud pack on her face, conditioner in her hair, and green tea brewing on the stovetop.

"What's she doing?" Christine asked, startling Traci.

"You can *hear* her?"

"Yeah. She's singing 'American Pie.' Cool song."

"Right." Traci failed to keep the sarcasm from her voice. It drove her crazy, the way her friends harped about her mother. But then, *they* hadn't heard "American Pie" two thousand times in Susan's high, slightly off-key soprano.

"I don't get your problem with your mom," Christine said, daring to swim into dangerous waters. "She's just different."

Traci started downstairs with the phone. Before she could think, she blurted out, "Maybe if she hadn't been so *different*, Dad wouldn't have left us."

"Oh, grow up, Traci! People get divorced all the time."

"Aren't you supposed to be on *my* side?" Traci couldn't help feeling hurt by the way Christine blew off her parents' divorce.

"I *am* on your side! I just think you should look on the bright side of this."

Reaching the bottom of the stairs, Traci paused and looked up in the direction of her room. She shivered.

Maybe she'd sleep on the couch tonight.

"Traci?"

"Um, the bright side, huh? And what would that be?"

"Wait."

When Christine started humming "American Pie" along with Susan, Traci heaved an aggravated sigh. "Listen," she interrupted, "I'm gonna go, okay?"

"Okay, but you gotta promise to call me if anything else weird happens tonight. Tell Mom it's an emergency."

"Okay."

"And don't forget to wear your lime-colored pants with that cute leather lace-up top. Kyle's standing in for Mr. Peachum."

"As if you'd call Mr. Landers Kyle to his face," Traci teased. "And I don't think he's that hot. Did you get a good look at the length of his nose hairs?"

"Yuck! You are so not funny, Trace! Who's looking at nose hairs? Now, those baby blues are worth looking at!"

"He's old."

"Not very."

"For me."

"Not me. 'Bye."

"'Bye!"

Traci grinned just thinking about Christine and Mr. Landers together. Christine was fifteen, and Mr. Landers was at least thirty. Twice their age. He'd get a ticket for just *looking* at them. Jailbait, as her daddy would say.

"Hey, honey! What's up?" Susan said from the kitchen doorway.

Bracing herself, Traci turned in that direction. Just as she'd known it would be, her mother's face was packed with a mud facial, and her hair was wrapped in a hot towel. She was blowing on her freshly painted nails. She grinned at Traci, her teeth a dazzling white against the backdrop of her mud-caked face.

Susan straightened in the doorway, her smile fading as she looked at Traci. "What's the matter, pumpkin? You look as if you've seen a ghost!"

Sometimes, Traci thought, swallowing hard, her mother could be darned perceptive.

"This metallic blue matches your eyes," Susan said as she carefully applied the nail polish to Traci's hopelessly short nails. "Don't you think?"

Traci shrugged impatiently. "Mom, this is serious! Have you heard anything I've told you?"

Without breaking concentration, Susan nodded. "You said that someone is playing a sick joke on you."

Her beautiful brown eyes flickered over Traci, then back to her task. She looked uncharacteristically thoughtful, reminding Traci that beneath that beautiful head of red hair, her mother had a brain.

"And it's definitely a sick joke, honey. You and Corky were like brother and sister."

Okay, Traci thought, maybe that was a slight exaggeration, considering the kissing she and Corky had done the winter before he died. Prudently, she kept quiet.

"Whoever's doing this e-mail thing obviously knows you two were close. What about Corky's friend — what's his name?"

The reminder gave Traci an ugly jolt. She hadn't thought about him! "Reggae Bruce?"

"Yeah, Reggae. He and Corky were tight, weren't they?"

"Yeah, but . . . " Traci shook her head, frowning. "I can't see Reggae doing something so mean, Mom. We didn't like each other, but we both loved Corky. I mean, he didn't *love* Corky, but you know what I mean."

Susan smiled faintly. "Yeah, I know what you mean. You can't call it love until you're at least twenty. Anything before that is considered queer."

"Nobody says 'queer' anymore, Mom." Traci waited while her mother switched hands. "Besides, I don't think Reggae would think it was very cool. He was with Corky when he drowned, remember?"

"Oh, yeah." Susan clucked her tongue. "That had to be traumatic for him."

"He didn't come to school for three months," Traci

said. Tears pricked her eyes. She blinked rapidly. "I don't think it's him."

"Who, then?"

Traci hesitated, then said, "Whoever it is knows about my birthmark."

Susan froze. She looked up, her eyes wide. "You mean, *that* one? The one on your . . . butt?"

"Yeah, that one." Traci felt heat creep into her face. "We, um, I mean, Corky painted me naked once. We were only about eight," Traci rushed on at the alarmed look on her mother's face. "His dad caught us and gave us a lecture."

Arching one fine brow, Susan asked with remarkable calm, "Anything else I should know about you and Corky?"

"No." Traci gave her head a hasty shake and stared at her bright blue nails. Christine would love the color; she hated it. It made her feel like an android. She thought about telling her mother about the ring she'd stolen long ago, but decided against it. She still couldn't admit that sin out loud.

"Honey, I think you should—"

Whatever wisdom Susan had been on the verge of imparting got interrupted by the unmistakable sound of a bell dinging. Susan looked up, startled. "What's that?"

Dumbfounded with shock, Traci said, "That's my computer! It lets me know when I've got . . . a . . .

message." Her voice trailed off to a horrified whisper.

The dinging stopped.

Traci's heart continued to pound. She had turned off the computer. She had *unplugged* the computer. And no way had she turned up the speakers to such a ridiculous volume.

Chapter Three

". . . and there, right on the computer screen, was a scrolling message. I always leave my screen saver on the scrolling marquee, but the message that was there wasn't the same message that *I* had created." If Christine's eyes grew any wider, Traci thought, they'd swallow her face. She knew exactly how she felt. "Mom thought I was playing a joke on her. She wouldn't believe me."

Christine stuck a fairly decent nail in her mouth and began to chew it to shreds. "What did the message say?"

"'Greetings, Bobcat.'"

"He's like a broken record," Christine mumbled. "So what did you do then?"

"I slept on the couch."

"Oh, God," Christine said, and amazingly enough her eyes *did* get bigger. She leaned forward to whisper in a panicky voice, "He's coming!"

For one insane moment Traci thought she meant Corky. Raw terror paralyzed her limbs. She unglued her tongue from the roof of her mouth and croaked, "How . . . how do you know?"

Christine's wide-eyed gaze shifted to a point beyond Traci's shoulder. She spoke, but her lips barely moved. "Because I'm looking at him, dummy. He's heading straight for us."

It finally dawned on Traci that her friend wasn't talking about Corky. She was talking about Brad

Davidson. Now a different kind of terror gripped Traci. Funny, she thought, she'd never figured herself for a coward until yesterday.

"What do you want me to do?" Christine whispered urgently. A huge fake smile spread over her pretty face, and her eyes rolled skyward.

Traci knew without turning around that the tall quarterback was standing behind her. Her mouth went bone dry and her palms began to sweat.

Stay, Traci mouthed to Christine.

"Can I talk to Traci alone, Christine?" Brad asked in his deep, sweet baritone.

So much for keeping Christine around for moral support, Traci thought, wondering if her heart was going to beat right out of her chest. Thank God she was young, or she'd be in trouble with the ol' ticker.

First a ghost talking to her through her computer, now Brad Davidson in the flesh.

And he wanted to speak to her alone.

She gulped and slowly turned, very aware that Christine had risen and was dragging her feet as she put some distance between them. Struggling to look casual and act casual, as if she hadn't played out this same scene a thousand times in her dreams, Traci completed the turn on the bench until she faced Brad.

Her gaze traveled slowly upward to his handsome face and green, green eyes. He wore his sandy-blond hair in that messy, I-went-to-bed-with-my-hair-wet style that was all the rage. Perhaps a little longer than most of the boys, but Traci liked it.

She liked *everything* about Brad Davidson, including his enviously long pale eyelashes.

She'd spoken to Brad before, of course, but never without people around to buffer the shock. Could she actually speak and make sense without Christine's silent moral support? Guess there was one way to find out. She opened her mouth.

And then Brad smiled.

Traci blinked, completely forgetting what she had been about to say to him.

His smile widened, revealing very white teeth. There was a small gap between his two front teeth. A flaw, Traci thought. But she even managed to find *that* cute.

"Hey," he said softly, his gaze dropping to her mouth.

Traci had a horrifying thought: What if she had peanut butter or jelly on her lips? If she had known Brad was going to approach her, she would have checked her mouth after lunch and reapplied her lipstick. Just in case, she licked her lips, trying to make the action look provocative instead of a sneaky search for lingering food. She'd watched her mother do it a dozen times.

But Traci knew her mother would never have forgotten to touch up her lipstick. Once Traci had sneaked into her mother's room while she was sleeping to see if she wore her lipstick to bed. She'd been relieved to find out that she didn't.

"Hey, yourself," she finally managed. Her voice came out husky and low, as if she had a frog in her throat. That wasn't her normal voice at all.

"So . . . when are we going to get together?"

Traci was so relieved that he hadn't said "hook up" instead of "get together." "Hook up" sounded more like something that applied to dogs than people. She flashed him a smile, silently praying she didn't have a piece of bread stuck between her teeth. From now on, she vowed, she was going to bring her toothbrush *and* her dental floss to school with her. "Are you asking me out?" *Stupid, stupid, stupid!* Of course he was asking her out! "I mean . . . you know what I mean."

"Your parents let you date, right?"

Okay, so there were a few things she liked about her mom, and this happened to be one of them. "Yes. It's just me and my mom, but she's cool with it as long as she meets you and—" Traci nearly chewed through her jaw. She couldn't believe how close she'd come to blurting out that her mother only let her date guys that gave off good "vibes." Susan didn't believe in ghosts, but she believed in vibes. Brad would think her mother nuts; he wouldn't be far from the truth.

"And?" he prompted, a little frown forming between his brows.

She hastily shook her head. "Oh, nothing. She just likes to meet the guys I go out with." She flushed. "I mean, I don't go out with a lot of guys or anything." Brad would be the second one, in fact, but she didn't want to sound like a total baby. Neither did she want to sound promiscuous. Oh, she didn't know *what* she wanted!

"That's cool with me. I live with my dad."

She had *known* they had something in common! Traci quivered with excitement. She had no doubt that her mother would feel the same good vibes that she was feeling about Brad Davidson. Traci frowned at the thought. She hoped Susan wouldn't get all flirty and silly and embarrass the heck out of her.

"Divorce sucks, huh?" she mumbled, hoping she wasn't getting too personal.

But Brad simply nodded before taking a seat on the bench beside her. Traci covertly glanced at her watch, then at Christine, who was standing a few feet away picking at her nails and shamelessly eavesdropping.

Three minutes till the bell rang.

"Yeah, it sucks, but I think I like it better than the fighting and shouting."

He was sharing with her—and this was their first conversation! Traci's heart did a happy little dance. Right then she couldn't imagine life getting any better.

Although it wasn't the total truth, Traci said, "Yeah, I hear you." He might be sharing with *her*, but she wasn't about to blow it by complaining about her mom. At least, not yet.

To think there might be a "yet" made her feel faint.

"So you wanna do something Friday night after the game? Maybe get some pizza at Charlie's?"

Charlie's was the local pizza place where a lot of people hung out on weekend nights. Traci didn't care if they spent the entire evening scrubbing commodes as long as she was with Brad. She nodded. "Sounds like fun. Um, would you mind coming inside and saying hi to my mom?"

Brad grinned. "Can't wait to meet her. My dad wants to meet you, too."

Traci swallowed hard. "You . . . you already told your dad about me?" she asked in a squeaky voice.

"Yeah." Brad's gaze drifted to her mouth again, giving Traci the impression he wanted to kiss her. "I've been thinking about you for a while now."

"You . . . you have?" Her voice hadn't lost that squeaky sound. She jumped as he slid his arm around her waist and tugged her closer. She had a choice: either push against him or lean into him.

She melted against him like a cube of ice on a sunburn. Her face felt hot as she gazed up at him, wavering between embarrassment and hope. Christine was watching, and probably a few other classmates by now. Did she want him to kiss her in front of every-one? And if he didn't, would she live through the day?

His mouth moved closer. She stared at his lips. Perfect lips. Handsome lips.

"I want to kiss you," he whispered in a low, deep voice. "But your friend is watching."

That's it, Traci thought, masking her disappointment. Christine would have to die. She managed a shaky laugh and tried to sit up straight. He reluctantly let her go. "She . . . she probably isn't the only one watching."

He grinned. "Probably not. I came from a big school where nobody really notices what anyone else is doing, so this is a huge change."

Traci had known he had transferred from Los Angeles to her hometown of Beachmont, Missouri. His experience living in a large city had been part of his appeal. She loved small-town life, but was curious about city life, too. She couldn't wait to hear more.

The bell rang. They both rose at the same time, and Traci got this warm, funny feeling in her belly as he kept his arm around her. Christine shot her a little pouty frown and stayed ahead of them, glancing back now and then as if she couldn't stand the suspense.

He left her in front of her classroom, where Christine was waiting. The moment he walked away, Christine said, "I'm so freaking jealous!"

She *sounded* jealous, too. Traci clung to that last ray

of warmth still swimming around in her belly as she turned to soothe her best friend. "I'm not going to start ignoring you, Christine, so don't start on me."

Christine laughed. "I didn't mean that I was jealous of *him*! I meant that I was jealous of *you*! That guy is a hunk, Trace." She let out a wistful, noisy sigh. "Now, if he just had a brother . . . "

It was Traci's turn to laugh.

The rest of the afternoon flew by in a hazy, happy fog. Traci couldn't wait to get home and check her e-mail. She just knew Brad was going to e-mail her, and she looked forward to spending a few hours talking to him. She preferred e-mail. That way she could talk to Christine on the phone while instant messaging to Brad on the computer. She didn't want her friend to feel left out, even though Christine had seemed pretty cool with the idea of her and Brad getting together.

Bursting into the house, she raced upstairs, switched on her computer, and ran back downstairs to fix a snack. She hummed as she waited for the Pop-Tarts to toast.

The moment the Pop-Tarts were done, Traci slapped them on a plate, grabbed a glass of milk, and raced back upstairs to her room. Belatedly, she realized her mother wasn't home, and vaguely remembered her saying something about signing up for beauty school. Nothing out of the ordinary for Susan; she changed careers as often as she changed hair color.

It wasn't until Traci had sat down in front of the screen that she remembered she was supposed to be frightened of her computer, and why. How could she have forgotten? But she knew the reason. *Brad* was the reason she'd forgotten.

Traci froze with the Pop-Tart in hand—a hand that began to tremble slightly. She clicked on her e-mail program, gasping at the number of new messages that appeared.

Fifty-two.

And fifty-one were from the Undertaker.

Chapter Four

The first new e-mail was from Brad, but Traci skipped over it as if he had never existed. Pop-Tart forgotten, she began clicking on the rest of the new messages, growing more astounded with each one.

They all said the same exact thing.

CAN YOU COME OVER TODAY?

How many times had Corky called and asked her that very question? Probably as many times as she had called and asked *him* to come over. Hundreds. Thousands.

It was insane. Crazy. Freaky.

Hysterical.

And that was exactly how she felt: hysterical. She was talking to a ghost. But how? And why? Why was Corky getting in touch with her *now*, just as she was starting a new relationship with Brad?

She shook her dazed head, realizing that her reasoning sounded as insane as the entire idea of Corky communicatng with her. Corky was dead. Drowned. Gone forever.

Her Pop-Tart fell to the floor and broke into a dozen pieces. Tears pricked her eyes. What if it were all true? What if Corky were a ghost, and were talking to her through e-mail?

She gulped and stared hard at the computer screen, as if it would give her the answers. What if she went over to Corky's house, into Corky's room, and he was there? In ghost form?

Was she losing her mind? Had her mother finally driven her insane?

"This is stupid," she muttered out loud. The sound of her own voice reassured her, so she continued talking to herself. "It's just a hoax, a nasty joke someone is playing on me. Corky hasn't come back from the dead. You've watched too many horror movies."

Resolutely, she clicked on Brad's e-mail, determined to ignore the idiot who was pretending to be Corky. Before she could focus on Brad's words, the bell began to ding over and over again. When she didn't immediately answer, messages began to pop up onto her screen, obliterating Brad's e-mail, overlapping again and again.

CAN YOU COME OVER TODAY?

Traci screamed and jabbed at the power button, shutting the computer down. The screen went black. She sat there staring at it, her eyes stretched wide, her heart beating like thunder.

The screen crackled with static electricity as it kicked back on without her help. Traci shoved away from the desk, sending her computer chair—and herself along with it—skittering across the room.

On the computer screen, the scrolling marquee began, the letters bigger and bolder than she remembered.

DON'T TURN ME OFF! CAN YOU COME OVER TODAY?

Over and over the words scrolled by. Faster and faster. Bigger and bolder. Traci slammed her eyes shut, but she could still see the flashing marquee from behind closed lids.

DON'T TURN ME OFF! CAN YOU COME OVER TODAY?

Slowly Traci rose, keeping her eyes closed as she felt her way to the door. She found it, then quickly opened it and went through, pulling it shut before she opened her eyes. She took several deep breaths, then turned and raced downstairs so fast she tripped on the bottom step and went sprawling on her butt. Shaking all over, she found some paper and a pen in a kitchen drawer and quickly wrote her mother a note, telling her she would be back in thirty minutes.

She paused, pen in hand. How long did it take to confirm the presence of a ghost? She shuddered and bit her lip. She badly wanted to call Christine, but knew that her friend couldn't leave the house until her parents got home. She had to baby-sit her rotten brothers.

What about Brad? Traci tapped the pen against her chattering teeth. And what would she tell him? *I'm going to my old boyfriend's house because I think he's come back from the dead?* Yeah, and he'd never give *her* another thought. He'd rightly think she was a lunatic.

Maybe she was. Maybe she really was losing her mind. But no, Christine had heard the bell dinging.

Her mother had heard it, too, even after Traci had disconnected the power to her computer.

She had to go and check it out, and it appeared she had no choice but to go alone.

Traci bit down hard on her pen to still her chattering teeth.

The grass needed mowing. Traci blinked back tears, remembering how Corky had mowed the lawn every Saturday. Mr. Evans had disappeared from their lives the year Corky turned nine, so Corky had become the man of the family. He'd taken good care of his mom, too.

And she had taken good care of Corky.

Traci felt sad as she approached the front door and rang the bell. She heard footsteps and knew that she'd caught Mrs. Evans at home. What would she say? How should she act? It had been over a year since she'd visited the woman. She felt guilty, knowing Mrs. Evans didn't have many friends in town. After her husband disappeared, she had become something of a recluse. She worked as a librarian, but other than going to work she didn't socialize much.

Corky blamed his father. He'd been very bitter about his desertion, and Traci could hardly blame him for that. She still saw her father and spent the weekend once in a while, but a part of her had never really gotten over his leaving.

The door opened and Traci stepped back, gathering her courage. "Hi, Mrs. Evans. Long time no see." Man, was she a dummy! *Long time no see.* How clichéd could she get?

"Traci!" Mrs. Evans lost her characteristic stern librarian look and smiled warmly at her. "Come in, come in. I was just about to have a bite of supper. Care to join me?"

Traci was tempted, but knew she was too nervous to eat. "Um, no thanks. I've already eaten." Lie number one. "I wondered if I could talk to you a minute?"

"Of course. Come right inside. I'll go turn the oven off so my lasagna won't dry out. You can wait for me in the living room."

Lasagna. Traci's mouth watered. She remembered Mrs. Evans's lasagna, all right. Why, she had probably lost ten pounds after she stopped eating Mrs. Evans's cooking.

In the living room, Traci tried to sit but found she was too antsy. She paced instead, throwing on a bright smile when Mrs. Evans returned from the kitchen.

"There," she said as she dusted her hands on her apron. She was a plump, pretty woman with black hair and dark eyes. Corky had looked a lot like her. "I've got supper on hold, so what did you have in mind? Just here for a nice chat?"

"Um." Traci twisted her fingers and got ready for lie

number two. "I was wondering . . . If it wouldn't be too much trouble, um, would you mind if I borrowed a few of Corky's computer games? They, um, have this new thing called burning a CD, so I could bring them back tomorrow." Traci held her breath as she watched Mrs. Evans. What if she made the woman cry? She'd never forgive herself!

Tears did sparkle in Mrs. Evans's eyes, but she was smiling right through them. "I'm sure he would love for you to have them. In fact, you can keep them. I certainly won't have any use for them." She laughed, but it was a sad sound. "Good grief, I know so little about computers." Her smile slipped a bit. "Corky threatened to teach me, but I kept making excuses. In the last few years I've gotten more comfortable with the ones at work, but I can't imagine ever playing computer games."

"I . . . I didn't mean to make you sad," Traci stammered. She felt awful, just awful. Maybe she should just leave—

"Don't you dare apologize!" Mrs. Evans scolded. "I'm not like some folks who just want to forget about their children because it's too painful to think about them. I don't want to *ever* forget about my Corky, and I don't expect you to, either, understand?"

"Yes, ma'am," Traci said meekly.

"You were his best friend in all the world, Traci."

Darn. The woman was going to make her cry if she

didn't stop! "He . . . he was my best friend, too. I miss him."

"Me too." Mrs. Evans drew in a shaky breath and let it out in a little chuckle. "If he's watching us now, he's probably laughing and calling us babies."

Traci summoned a tremulous smile, thinking Mrs. Evans was probably right, but the poor woman couldn't know how very close to the truth she might be. She shot a nervous glance at the hallway leading to Corky's room.

It looked dark and sinister. Traci shivered.

Mrs. Evans misinterpreted her actions. "Oh, you're anxious to get to those games, aren't you? And here I just keep rambling away. Go ahead, darling," she said softly. "Help yourself to anything you want."

She hesitated, not wanting Corky's mom to think she was a selfish brat just after the games. She wanted Mrs. Evans to know that she still thought about Corky, and missed him like crazy. *Not enough to want him back as a ghost, though,* she thought, and shivered again.

"Are you cold, Traci? I thought it was unseasonably warm for October. Even the bees are coming back out. Not coming down with a chill, are you?"

"Um, no, ma'am. I was just thinking about something." Which wasn't a lie, only it was some*body*, not some*thing*. A naughty ghost in particular. Impulsively she said, "Won't you come with me?" Actually, she

46

was a coward and didn't want to go into that room alone.

"Oh, I don't think so." Mrs. Evans looked away. More tears sparkled in her eyes. "I haven't reached that point yet, I'm afraid. You go ahead without me."

Great, Traci thought, swallowing a knot of fear. She'd just go right into that room and see for herself there was no ghost. She didn't really think there would be, did she? Traci gave an inward snort of derision. Of course not. Just someone who had stumbled across Corky's diary or something.

Traci couldn't resist a smile at the thought of Corky keeping a diary. Corky had been all boy. He would have thought keeping a diary a definite girl thing.

Slowly she walked down the hall to his room, aware of Mrs. Evans watching her. The doorknob to Corky's bedroom was cold. Was that strange? she wondered, swallowing hard again. It was warm inside the house. Why would his doorknob be cold? *You're just being paranoid, you ninny*, her inner voice sneered. *Just get your butt inside the room and see for yourself that Corky's not there.*

She took a deep breath and opened the door. The first thing she noticed was the musty smell. She wrinkled her nose, thinking Mrs. Evans would eventually have to air out the room. Stepping across the threshold, Traci kept her hand on the knob as she surveyed the empty room.

No ghost; just a boy's room with a boy's things. There was a twin bed covered with a handmade quilt Traci remembered watching Mrs. Evans make. On the right side of the bed was a chest of drawers, a set of weights, and a small night table and lamp. Traci's gaze skimmed the walls that were covered in posters of the Undertaker. How proud Corky had been of them. He'd vowed that when we was old enough he was going to be a pro wrestler with his own unforgettable name.

His dreams had ended the day he and Reggae decided to go swimming in Crawford Lake.

Finally her attention fell on the computer to the left of Corky's bed. It was eerie looking at it and knowing that Corky would never sit in his chair again, would never send her funny e-mail or forward the address to an interesting Web site he'd found while surfing.

A lone tear trickled down her cheek. Traci sniffed and whisked it away with her tongue. She had to get herself together before she fell completely apart. Corky had been gone two years; surely that was enough time to get over someone.

"Shut the door, Bobcat."

Traci choked on a scream. "Wh-what?" It had been Corky's voice, or someone who could sound exactly like him.

"Shut the door, will you? I don't think Mom could

stand the strain, do you? She doesn't look so good."

Corky again. His voice . . . but where was he?

Scanning the room with bulging eyes, Traci slowly shut the door. She didn't want to—oh, no. But she also didn't want Mrs. Evans to hear her—or him. If there was indeed a him. "Where . . . where are you?" She'd play along with the full knowledge that this was an elaborate, not-very-funny hoax. Nevertheless, she kept her voice slightly above a whisper.

"Over here, on the bed. I haven't figured out how to make myself visible yet. I can make a few sparks, and do a few tricks using the power lines—that's how I turned your computer back on—but that's about it."

Traci swayed where she stood. She stuck her hands behind her to brace herself against the door. Her heart had lodged somewhere between her tonsils and her voice box.

"Come on, Trace! You've never been a coward. Don't start wimping out on me now. I thought you'd never come over."

Coward? Her? Absolutely, and she wasn't ashamed of the fact. "You . . . you . . . " It was no use. She wasn't getting much past the heart in her throat. She tried unsuccessfully to swallow it. Corky was a ghost, and he was talking to her as if he'd never died.

"Man, I see you've lost most of your baby fat. Guess chasing boys will do that to you."

It was Corky all right. He'd always had the knack

for ruffling her feathers. She licked her dry-as-a-bone lips and tried to talk again. "You—" Okay, so she had a voice, but it sounded like it belonged to someone else. "Is . . . is that really you?"

"Who else would be in my room?" he countered a little sarcastically. "Other than you, that is. I heard Mom giving away my stuff. I can't believe she'd do that."

Traci felt compelled to defend Mrs. Evans. "You've been . . . *gone* two years, Corky." Did calling him by name mean she believed he was real?

"You mean dead, don't you?"

He didn't sound upset about the fact. Traci resisted the urge to pinch herself. Maybe she'd fallen asleep at home and was dreaming this entire episode.

"Nah, you ain't dreaming, Bobcat."

Traci gave a start. "You can read my mind?"

"No, but I can read your expression, and it's practically screaming 'I'm dreaming.' Hey, I'm a poet and didn't know it."

"Not only a poet, but a ghost." Traci wanted to hear him confirm it. If she was being filmed, she would simply die.

"That's right, I'm a ghost."

To her horror, she heard the bed springs creak as if someone had sat on the bed, or . . . or . . .

"Don't scream, okay? I'm coming your way."

Traci didn't consider screaming at all. She opened

the door and fled as if her life depended on it.

"Hey! Come back here! I can't believe you're leaving after all the trouble I went through to get you—"

The voice got louder. Traci cast a terrified glance over her shoulder as she ran down the hall. Was he coming after her? Could he leave his room? Was he really a ghost?

She turned around just in time to see the wall looming in front of her.

It was too late to stop.

Chapter Five

Her head hurt, but that wasn't the worst of her problems.

Mrs. Evans insisted on driving her home. Traci had protested that she could walk, reminding the concerned woman that her house was just down the street. She could actually *see* it from Mrs. Evans's front porch.

Mrs. Evans would not budge.

She also insisted on coming inside with Traci once they reached Traci's house. Traci groaned out loud at this, noticing her mother's car parked in the garage. Corky's mom and *her* mom were as different as night and day, and had always maintained an awkward relationship.

To her intense relief, her mother was nowhere to be seen or heard as they entered the house. Traci turned to Mrs. Evans and told lie number three. "Mom's not home, but I promise you I'll be fine." She gingerly fingered the lump on her forehead. "I've had bigger bumps than this and survived."

"I'm sure you have, darling," Mrs. Evans said, still looking concerned. "But I don't like leaving you—"

"I'm going to lie down." Lie number four.

"Maybe I should take you to the emergency room just as a precaution. You might have suffered a concussion."

Lie number five. "Mom's had some nursing experience."

"Oh?" Mrs. Evans looked skeptical. "Are you sure?"

"Believe me, I'm sure." Didn't volunteer work count? She stopped counting her lies. If the woman didn't leave soon her nose was going to start growing. At the very least she'd start tripping over her own lies. She'd never been very good at lying.

Ever so slowly Mrs. Evans edged toward the door. Traci moved with her, hoping to force her along.

"Okay," she said reluctantly. "I'll go, but I'm calling you later to see if you're okay."

"Okay." Traci winced visibly. Just as she'd planned, Mrs. Evans saw her reaction and hurriedly left so that she could "lie down." As if she could lie still after what she'd been through! *Ha!* She'd be lucky if she slept more than a few seconds after that terrifying experience. "This is so messed up," she whispered.

"Trace? Is that you?"

Thank God she had shut the front door before her mother called out to her from the master bedroom downstairs. Prepared to answer a dozen rapid-fire questions about her injury, Traci trudged to her mother's room.

The moment her mother saw her, she jumped from her bed and rushed to her. "What happened to you, honey?"

Traci stared at the big red bump on her mother's forehead, momentarily speechless. Faintly, she said, "I ran into a wall. What happened to *you*?"

"I had an altercation with a car," Susan said with a grimace. She was holding a bag of frozen pizza rolls. "Here, try this. Watch out, it might hurt."

Taking the bag, Traci gingerly pressed it to the bump. "Ouch! You were in an accident?"

Susan led her to the bed and pushed her down. "Yes, and the creep swears it was all *my* fault."

"Was it?" Traci knew by the way her mother narrowed her eyes that she should have used more tact.

"No, it was not. He pulled out in front of me and I couldn't stop in time."

Her head was throbbing. She wanted to take some asprin and lie down, but not in *that* room. "So why is he saying it's *your* fault?"

"He claims that if I hadn't been speeding he would have had plenty of time to get out of my way."

When Susan's gaze slid from Traci's, Traci heaved a weary sigh. "Mom, were you speeding?"

"I hate it, pumpkin, when you assume the worst about me." When Traci merely lifted an eyebrow — cautiously — Susan caved. "Oh, all right. Yes, I was speeding, but only because I dropped my nail file. When I tried to pick it up, I inadvertently stepped on the gas pedal."

"You were filing your nails while you were driving?" Traci couldn't believe what she was hearing. She felt like the mother scolding the daughter, instead of the other way around.

"Of course not! I had just broken a nail and was trying to repair it before I lost the whole damned thing. It was an accident, one anyone could make. *He* pulled out in front of me, and that's that. It was his fault."

"What did the cops say about it?"

Susan shrugged. "They said we'd have to fight it out in court, which I fully intend to do. Mr. Davidson's gonna find out he bit off more than he could chew by messing with me."

A wave of dizziness washed over Traci. She shook her head to clear it, then stuck her fingers in her ears and gave them a vigorous wiggle. Maybe she *did* suffer from a concussion, because she thought her mother had said Mr. *Davidson*, and that couldn't be right . . . no way could that be right.

But just to be on the safe side . . . "Who did you say you ran into?"

"I didn't run into anyone," Susan argued, sounding peeved all over again. "He pulled out in front of me, and his name is Jed . . . Fred . . . something or other Davidson. He's a businessman, said he was a lawyer." Susan snorted. "I think he was lying just to scare me. Well, I'm not scared, so he can just get over himself."

Ted Davidson.

As badly as it hurt, Traci leaned forward and put her head between her knees. She didn't care to pass out and hit her head again.

Susan forget her own problems instantly. "Oh, pumpkin! Do you think you should see a doctor? That's a nasty bump."

Traci glanced up, staring at the identical bump on her mother's forehead. She started laughing and couldn't stop.

"I don't know what you find so funny," her mother said, sounding peeved again. "That maniac driver could have gotten me killed."

When Traci was able to speak again, she wiped her streaming eyes and said, "Sorry. I just couldn't help myself."

Susan gave an injured sniff. "I still don't see what you find so funny."

But Traci couldn't explain, because she didn't want her mother to know the truth.

Unless there were two Ted Davidsons in her small town, that "maniac driver"—as her mother so fondly referred to him—happened to be Brad Davidson's father.

What a mess!

Traci locked herself in the bathroom and called Brad from her cell phone. No way was she going into her room until she had time to think—or see a shrink. Oh, God, she was beginning to *sound* like Corky, with his stupid rhymes! As she waited for someone to pick up, she glanced down the hall to make certain her mother's door remained shut. Susan had taken a pain pill the ER doctor had prescribed, so Traci was banking on her mother's sleeping for a while.

"Hello?"

Traci jumped at the sound of Brad's voice, although she should have been expecting it. "Hi. It's Traci."

"Hey! I was just thinking about you."

He sounded pleased. *Good.* "Um, I was wondering if you'd like to hang out a little while." Traci bit her lip; she'd just broken her own rule, the one where she let the guy do the asking.

He hesitated just long enough to make her heart stop in its tracks. "Sure. Can you give me fifteen minutes? My old man's on my case about this trig test I've got tomorrow. Sheesh. You'd think *he* was the one taking it."

"Fifteen minutes is fine." *Here goes nothing!* "Can you, um, pick me up at the end of my street?" Silence. At least a moment or two. Not a good sign. Traci squeezed the phone so hard she thought she heard something crack. She rushed ahead before he had the opportunity to respond. "My mother's not feeling well, so I don't want to wake her with the doorbell."

"You could watch out the window for me," he suggested, still sounding hesitant.

Normally she went bonkers for the strong, honest

58

type. But this wasn't one of those times. "She has very keen hearing." Which wasn't a lie. Her mother could hear a crumb drop in the kitchen from her bedroom.

After another long, suspenseful silence, Brad said, "Okay, I'll pick you up there . . . if you're sure you won't get into trouble."

"I won't." She wouldn't, either, because she was determined her mother wouldn't know about it. Oh, her mother wouldn't care if she went out with a boy; Traci just didn't want her to know about Brad at all. Not yet, anyway. Maybe not ever after today.

"See ya in fifteen," Brad said.

"Okay. 'Bye." Traci stuck the phone in the little purse she kept clipped to her belt loop, then tiptoed to her mother's door. She listened closely, hearing nothing. Satisfied, she returned to the bathroom to brush her teeth and comb her short blond hair.

If Brad kissed her tonight, she wanted to be prepared.

Fifteen minutes later, Traci stood at the corner of Wayne and McGovern streets waiting for Brad. The house where Corky had lived was a few houses down, but she felt as if it were directly behind her. Was he watching her? Was she crazy?

She tried *not* to think about Corky the ghost or the accident her mother had had with Brad's father. She tried not to think about *anything* but Brad and his gorgeous green eyes.

But when Brad pulled up in his father's car, Traci

could do nothing but gawk at the hunter-green wreckage that had once been a sweet, sleek BMW. Brad reached across the passenger seat and opened the door for her, grinning at her astounded expression.

"Don't look so scared. I wasn't driving, Dad was."

Still speechless, Traci slid into the car and pulled the battered door shut. She had to slam it twice before it stayed closed. Mouth dry, she stared at the cracked windshield. "What . . . what happened?" She knew, of course, but she wanted to hear Ted Davidson's side of the story. Chances were it would not resemble her mother's story.

"Got it?"

"I think so." Traci held her breath as Brad leaned very close to her to check the door for himself. He smelled good, like soap and something she couldn't quite put her finger on. Cologne, maybe? The good stuff that came from fancy department stores, not like the cheap perfume her mother bought. They lived mostly on the alimony and child support they got from her father, but when her mother was between jobs, that wasn't always enough for the finer things in life.

Like expensive perfume.

"Dad was in an accident today," he said as he put the car into drive and accelerated slowly. "Said some ditzy redhead plowed into him."

Traci thought her mother was a little on the crazy side, but she never thought of her as ditzy. She opened her mouth to stick up for her mom, but Brad continued before she could get a word out.

"Just between you and me, I think the old man drives too crazily. He's always in a hurry and takes unnecessary risks."

Somewhat soothed by Brad's older-than-his-years comment, Traci let out an inward sigh, glad that she hadn't said something she'd regret. "So you think maybe the accident was your dad's fault?" From the corner of her eye—she didn't dare look at him—she saw Brad frown in thought.

"Hard to say. He admits that he pulled out in front of her, but he swears he would have had plenty of time to get out of her way if she had been driving the speed limit."

"Sounds like maybe they were *both* at fault," Traci said, and meant it.

Brad snorted. "Tell that to my dad. He's a lawyer, and he doesn't back down for anybody or from anything."

Traci winced. So he *was* a lawyer, which meant her mother probably didn't have a chance of winning the case. But she couldn't explain that to her mother without revealing that she was dating the son of said lawyer.

What a disaster. It just wasn't fair!

"So, you gonna tell me how you got that bump on your head?"

Dryly, and with perfect honesty, Traci said, "I ran into a wall. How's that for clichéd?"

Brad glanced at her. "You're serious?"

"I'm serious."

"Why were you running?"

A perfectly logical question, Traci mused. "Take my word for it, you don't want to know." *I saw a ghost*, she wanted to shout. She was longing to talk to someone about it, but she was afraid nobody would believe her, least of all Brad, who didn't really know much about her.

"Wanna stop at Sonic Drive-In and get a soda?" Brad asked.

"Sure—" Traci's cell phone began to vibrate against her hip. She'd forgotten she'd switched it over so the ringing wouldn't wake her mom. "Probably Christine," she muttered by way of an apology as she fumbled to retrieve it. Her seat belt was in the way, so she had to undo it to get the phone. By the time she answered it, it had vibrated five separate times. "Hello?" she said breathlessly, fully expecting to hear Christine's bratty brothers shouting in the background. They loved to taunt their sister, especially when she was on the phone.

"Did I interrupt something?"

At the sound of Corky's bemused voice, Traci uttered a sharp scream and dropped the phone. It clattered to the floor of the car and landed near her foot.

"You all right?" Brad asked, sounding concerned.

No, she was definitely not all right! She stared at the phone as if it were a coiled snake about to strike. Carefully she inched her foot away from the phone.

"Aren't you going to pick it up?"

"Um, yeah. Right." She didn't move until she heard Corky's voice calling her name. A quick glance at Brad revealed that he, too, had heard the voice. So she wasn't crazy.

And now Brad knew the voice on the phone was male. If she didn't pick it up and talk to him, Brad might become suspicious. Clandestine meetings at street corners . . . strange boys calling. A bump on her head.

She hastily grabbed up the phone and put it to her ear before Corky said something she would regret Brad hearing. Her hand was shaking, but she hoped Brad couldn't see it. "What . . . what do you want?" Her creepy, hoarse voice had returned!

"I don't remember you being so mean, Trace."

She ground her teeth. Was she actually talking to Corky? She still couldn't believe it. Maybe that was why she couldn't be nice. "Get to the point. I'm busy."

"Isn't he a little too old for you?" Corky asked in a fatherly tone that immediately ruffled Traci's feathers.

"He's just seventeen." Why in heck was she defending herself to a ghost? And why in heck was Corky acting like he was her father?

"So why did he pick you up at the street corner instead of your house?"

"How did you know that?"

"Because I saw you from my bedroom window."

Traci swallowed hard. He was right; he would have been able to see from his bedroom window. "It's none of your business," she said, at a loss for words. What did one say to a ghost? *Buzz off?*

"I thought you'd be happy to see me . . . Bobcat."

He sounded as if he were pouting, and that sounded exactly like the Corky of old. Nevertheless, the conversation was bizarre, and that was putting it mildly. "Look, can we discuss this later?"

"I don't know. Can we? Will you *talk* to me later?"

"Yes." As she jabbed the Off button, she glanced up to discover they had pulled into a slot at Sonic, one of the few drive-in restaurants that had remained steadfast in their area. Brad was looking at her as if she'd grown two heads.

"Mind telling me what that was all about?" he asked.

Chapter Six

The way Traci figured it, she had two choices: She could tell Brad one whopper of a lie—they weren't, after all, officially dating—or she could tell the truth with a slight omission.

She opted for the truth with a small, yet important omission. "That was, um, Corky Evans. He's . . . we've been friends since we were little." Not one single lie had she told. Yet.

"He sounded as if he didn't approve of our going out."

Well. That. "He's a little overprotective sometimes. Like . . . like an older brother." She cleared her throat and studied the cracked windshield. Her mother had done that in her heroic efforts to save a nail. She blinked, wondering how her life had suddenly become so complicated.

"He sounded more like your father," Brad pointed out, still staring at her intently.

Traci wanted to squirm. She totally agreed with Brad, so what could she say? "When I said a *little* overprotective, I meant a *lot* overprotective. He's just . . . just that way."

"He cares about you," Brad said softly, as if he were stating an observation.

"Not like you think," Traci hastened to correct him. "Just in a brotherly way."

"What does he have against me? Have I met him?"

Not in this lifetime, Traci thought. "No, you haven't

met him." She hesitated, trying to put herself in Corky's place, trying to see what might worry him about Brad. "He doesn't really have anything against you; it's just that . . . well, you're from a big city, for starters."

"Ah."

"And your dad's a lawyer, which means that in *his* eyes you're a rich kid." She was making it up as she went along, but the more she spoke, the easier it got. Mainly because her—Corky's—reasoning could possibly be considered logical, if Corky *had* truly been her older brother. "And you *are* a year older than me."

"Okay. I'll give him that one."

She shot him a quick glance to see if he was making fun of her. He wasn't. "Plus, you drive."

"Now *that* one I don't get."

Her face got hot just thinking about what she was about to say. "Boys who drive can take girls they date to Widow's Point."

"I take it this is a place where couples go to hook up?"

The fact that he hadn't known about Widow's Point after living in Beachmont for six months was a big plus in his favor. She couldn't wait to tell Corky.

Wait. What was she saying? Was she accepting the fact that he was real? Or not real, but a ghost? *Good grief.* Remembering that Brad was waiting for an answer, she nodded. "Yeah, that's what most couples . . . do."

She tilted her chin before adding bravely, "I've never been." Actually, she had, but not in the way it counted. She and Christine had ridden their bikes to the point last year to spy on the couples parked there.

They hadn't been able to see through the steamed windows, but it had been an eye-opener just the same. She wondered if Brad would want to take *her* there, and if she would let him. Maybe, after she got to know him a *lot* better, and if he just wanted to kiss. She didn't think she was ready for anything else.

What was she thinking? After today he would probably decide she was too confusing to bother with. Lost in thought, she nearly screamed as Brad leaned forward and slid his arm around her neck. Slowly he tugged her to him until they were nearly nose to nose.

Traci forgot to breathe. Was this it? Was he about to kiss her for the first time? Her heart fluttered like a wild thing as she waited.

Soft and serious, he said, "You can tell Corky that I would never, ever force you to do something you didn't want to do."

His warm breath melted her resistance like butter left in the sun.

"And you can tell Corky that coming from a big city doesn't make me a monster."

His gaze dropped to her mouth. Traci's heart did a giddy little somersault. Corky who? What was he saying? Something about telling Corky . . .

"You can also tell Corky that the BMW was a repo my dad just happened to luck into, and that my dad is a public defender, and public defenders don't make anything, so that puts us in the low-to middle-income bracket. Can I kiss you?"

Traci blinked. She'd been hypnotized by the low, sweet sound of his voice, so his unexpected question was slow to sink in. When it did, her eyes went wide. "You . . . you don't have to ask me," she stammered. Her face was getting warm again; she wondered if he noticed. She also couldn't help wondering if Brad would notice that she wasn't exactly an expert in the art of kissing.

Just when she was certain she couldn't have put a stick of gum between their mouths, the guy in the car next to them laid on his horn.

They both jumped as if someone had goosed them in the ribs. She banged her elbow on the door behind her, and Brad banged his on the steering wheel. They both said, "Ow!"

Brad grimaced, placing his finger where his lips had nearly been. "This place is too public anyway," he said with a sheepish grin that totally endeared him to Traci. "When we kiss for the . . . first time, I want it to be when we're alone, don't you?"

Hiding her disappointment, Traci nodded. She agreed with him, yet she didn't. She wanted him to kiss her so badly her stomach ached. But Brad was right; the drive-in was too public. To be honest, she had totally forgotten everyone and everything in those few expectant seconds when Brad had been on the verge of kissing her.

"So," Brad said, his voice resuming his normal baritone, "you've told me what your friend Corky thinks of me. What about Christine?"

Traci grinned. "She thinks you are hot, hot, hot!"

Brad wiggled his eyebrows, making her giggle. "Maybe I should ask *her* out." He was clearly teasing.

Laughing, Traci shook her head. "No, no. She would absolutely have a heart attack, and I wouldn't want to lose my best friend." She'd already lost one best friend. The thought sobered her.

"You're thinking of something sad," Brad guessed shrewdly. "Care to share?"

Surprised, Traci blurted out before she could think, "I thought hot guys like you were supposed to be self-centered and into talking about themselves."

This time it was Brad's turn to blush. Traci stared at his flushed cheeks in amazement. That blush was the sweetest thing Traci had ever seen, and told her more about Brad than she probably could have ferreted out in a month's worth of dates.

He wasn't conceited, and he wasn't self-centered. How had she gotten so lucky? *Whoa, girl. He isn't yours yet, so don't count your chickens before they hatch. If he finds out you've been talking to a ghost, he'll be gone so fast you'll see nothing but the soles of his Nikes.*

"Thanks for the compliment . . . I think." He grinned and fiddled with her hair for a moment—long enough to make her breathless. "And for the challenge. Now I'm determined to prove to you that I'm not like most guys, hot or otherwise."

Traci wished fervently that she could make the cars on either side of them disappear so that she could lean forward and show him exactly how happy she was that he wasn't like other guys.

"Want a Coke or something?" Brad asked, looking at her as if he couldn't bear to take his eyes from her.

"Um, sure. I'll take a diet something." He rolled his eyes, showing her that he *could* be typical. Strangely, the knowledge relaxed her. She wanted him to be different, but not *too* different.

"As if you need to worry about your weight," he said, sounding as if he meant it.

Okay. Now she was *really* falling in love. Corky had said earlier that he noticed she'd lost *some* of her baby fat. Corky was right; she did have five or six pounds she could do without, but bless Brad's sweet heart for not noticing.

Brad ordered their sodas, then rolled up the window again. He had left the car running and the air conditioning was heaven. So were the leather seats, for that matter. Traci's dad drove a nice car, but it wasn't a BMW. She'd heard him complain more than once that he wasn't living the lifestyle his job as new car salesman required because of all the alimony he had to pay Susan.

"I've told you what my dad does for a living. What does your dad do?"

The question startled Traci, since she'd just been thinking about her dad. "He's a car salesman."

"See him much?"

"Yeah. He lives in Holcomb—a town about thirty miles from here—so I spend the weekend with him whenever I like. He's . . . he's cool."

"And your mom? Does she work?"

"She's between jobs, but she just signed up for beauty school. What does your mom do?" She caught a hint of sadness in his eyes and mentally kicked herself.

"She stayed in Los Angeles. She runs her own bakery there. That's one of the reasons my parents split, because she worked nearly opposite the hours my dad worked."

He was waiting, Traci realized with a sinking heart, for her to tell him the reason *her* parents split. He'd been honest; she could do no less with a clear conscience. "I think my parents split because they were too different."

"They say opposites attract," Brad said.

"Yes, well . . . I think in this case it was a matter of them being *too* opposite. Mom's a little weird."

"Weird?" His eyebrows went up again. "Weird as in she turns into a werewolf when there's a full moon?"

He was teasing her again. Traci decided she liked it. "Weird as in she listens to the same music and wears the same style of clothing as me. You've heard of the expression 'you're as young as you feel'? Well, my mom feels *very* young." Traci sighed, then added, "Sometimes I feel like she's more of an older sister than a mother."

"She sounds pretty cool to me," Brad said.

"Yeah, well. That's what everyone says. I think the final straw for my dad was the day she talked the workers at the fan factory into going on strike for better wages."

"Sounds noble to me."

Traci looked at him without smiling. "She didn't even work there, and she incited a riot and got arrested. Connie Lee dislocated his collarbone, Sam Dempsey broke his big toe, and Lucy Jenkins caught her hair on fire when Sam dropped his cigar in it to hold his broken toe and howl."

"Oh." Brad's lips twitched.

"Yeah, *oh*, and that's not the worst of it. Some of Dad's friends owned shares in the factory. I think at first Dad loved Mom because she was so brave and adventurous, but after a while he got tired of it."

"You blame her the most," Brad said.

She thought about denying it, but decided in the

end that she might as well come clean. "Yeah, I guess I do. It's hard to blame Dad when she was the one always doing crazy things that embarrassed him."

"Sounds like she was just being herself, and he tried to change her."

Traci had never thought of it that way. She was mulling it over when her cell phone began to jiggle. She tried to ignore it, but Brad saw the vibration.

"Aren't you going to get that?" He shot her a teasing grin. "It might be Big Brother checking to make sure the big bad wolf didn't eat you."

He was too close to the truth for Traci to find it funny. Bracing herself, she took out her phone and answered it. "Hello?"

"You've got to come over," Corky whispered. "Right now."

His urgent tone spiked a surge of adrenaline into her bloodstream. For a moment she forgot that he was a ghost. She was talking to Corky, her dear childhood friend, and he sounded as if he were in trouble. "What's going on?"

"He's back!" Corky whispered loudly.

"Who?"

"My father, Trace. He's come home."

Chapter Seven

"Traci, have you been drinking?"

Traci closed her eyes and counted to ten very slowly. After the day she'd had, she wasn't in the mood for Christine's twisted sense of humor. "No, Christine, I have not been drinking. You know I hate the taste of alcohol. Everything I just told you happened today."

"Wow. I mean, if you think about it, really think about it, your story is almost too bizarre to be believed."

"Are you calling your best friend a liar?"

"You mean your second best friend."

"What?"

Christine sounded upset, which Traci did *not* need. "Well, if Corky's back from the grave, and he was your best friend before I came along . . . "

"Ha. Ha. Ha. You *are* kidding, right?" As Traci waited for Christine to answer, she cracked the bathroom door and looked carefully down the hall.

Susan had awakened from her nap ravenous and had gone to get a pizza. She didn't appear to be back yet. Traci eased the door shut again.

"Okay. Let me see if I got this straight. Corky e-mailed you and asked you to come over."

"Yeah. About fifty times."

"You go to his house and into his room, and he talks to you, but you can't see him."

"Uh-huh." The hairs on the back of Traci's neck rose in remembrance.

"The moment he says he's coming your way, you take off and run straight into the wall at the end of the hall, knocking yourself senseless."

"You're getting the picture." She gingerly fingered the subsiding knot on her forehead. It no longer matched the one on her mother's head; that one hadn't gone down.

"Mrs. Evans brings you home. You discover that your mother has an identical bump on *her* head from an accident she had with Brad's father. You coerce Brad into taking you for a ride. He picks you up in his father's wrecked BMW, and while you're riding around Corky the teenage ghost calls you on your cell phone."

"You got it."

"You hang up. He calls back telling you that his long-lost father has come home."

"Can you imagine how he feels about that? I mean, his father just walked out on them without a backward glance, and now he shows up as if five years hadn't gone by." Traci could easily imagine how *she* would feel: angry, hurt, and definitely suspicious of the deserting father's motives.

"Traci?"

"Yeah?"

"Are you *positive* you don't have a concussion? Because that's one twisted story, girlfriend."

Traci lost her cool. "I do not have a stupid concussion! If you don't believe me, then call Brad and ask him. He can confirm that I got those calls."

"Okay. Let's say I believe you. What are you going to do?"

"About which problem?" There were several. Didn't Christine see that?

"Let's start with the wreck. Are you going to tell Brad about your mom?"

"No." *Uh-uh. Definitely not.*

"Well then, are you going to tell your mom about Brad?"

"No." *Double definitely not.*

"How about Corky and his dilemma? You going to help him out?"

At the end of an explosive sigh, Traci said, "I don't see how I can help him! I can't just march in and tell his father that his son, who's a ghost, doesn't want him in his house!"

"Yeah," Christine said in a matter-of-fact voice, "you'd think Corky could do his own haunting, scare his old man away."

"I don't think he's quite mastered the art of spooking anyone." Nobody besides her, anyway, and he'd done a good job of that! "He can't even make himself visible yet."

"He could call his old man on the phone and scare the beejesus out of him like he did you."

It wasn't a half-bad idea. Beat the heck out of her storming in and demanding he leave. Mrs. Evans would call an ambulance for certain, or whoever they called these days when a person went bonkers.

"If you go over there, I want to go," Christine announced.

Brave girl, Traci thought. But she'd heard that unmistakable quaver in her friend's voice, so she knew Christine was a big fat fake. "Why?"

"Well, because I've never seen a real live ghost before, Trace! Do you have any idea how mind-blowing the thought of meeting a real ghost is? Aren't you the teeniest bit excited about this phenomenon?"

Traci didn't hesitate. "No, I'm not. What I am is freaked out. Why is he back? What does he want? How long is he going to stay? Those are the questions I want answered."

"We could get him on film—"

"We're not doing the *Blair Witch* thing, Christine, so forget it. And might I remind you those kids were never found?"

"Corky's not a witch; he's a ghost, and he's your best friend."

"We are not having this conversation."

"Yes, we are."

"No, we're not."

"Yes, we are," Christine continued stubbornly. "I want to go with you."

"I'm *not* going back over there!" Traci shouted, then clamped a hand over her mouth. On the off chance her mother had returned without her knowledge, she did not want her to hear. She'd rush her only child straight to a shrink, possibly lock her in a nuthouse.

Christine was unperturbed by her outburst. "Maybe his father returning is the reason Corky's here. If you don't help him, then he'll keep hanging around."

The possibility both terrified and delighted her. She couldn't deny that she had missed Corky in a major way. Christine was a great friend, but with Corky it had been . . . almost as if they were in tune with each other. Corny, yes, but true. She had looked out for him and Corky had looked out for her, just as he'd looked out for his mother.

What if Christine was right and Corky had come back to take care of his mother one last time? Getting rid of his deadbeat father before he hurt his mother again would probably rank right up there on the priority lists of Things a Ghost Would Do.

"Trace? Hey, what's the worst thing that could happen if you went back? You seem to have accepted the fact that Corky has returned, so what are you afraid of?"

What *was* she afraid of? Was she afraid of having to go through the pain of losing Corky again when it came time for him to move on? Or was she just plain frightened of the fact that he was a ghost?

Very good questions.

Unfortunately, she didn't know the answers.

* * * *

Corky looked nothing like his father.

Traci stared at the man who had answered the door. He looked older than she remembered, and there were a few lines around his mouth that hadn't been there before. Maybe they were guilt lines, she thought, wondering if there were such a thing.

Christine pinched her sharply on the arm. She jerked and glared at her friend. Christine ignored her.

"Hi! We're, um, here to see Mrs. Evans. She around?"

The blond-haired man never cracked a smile. "Hello, Traci. You're all grown up, I see. Come in."

So he remembered her. Traci still didn't trust him. How could she? The man had left his wife and child without a good-bye or anything. As far as she was concerned, he had a lot of nerve coming back. Poor Corky! And poor Mrs. Evans, if she was about to be taken in by this bum a second time.

They waited in the foyer as the man disappeared through a doorway to the right of the hall, which Traci knew was the kitchen. She couldn't count how many times she and Corky had sat in that sunny kitchen at the old scarred worktable and dipped cookies into their milk, or took turns stacking Honeycomb cereal until the tall columns tottered and fell.

A sharp pang of nostalgia hit Traci. Tears pricked her eyes again. Apparently, she thought, blinking rapidly in an effort to get rid of the moisture, she couldn't come into Corky's house without reliving painful, yet happy memories.

"Are you okay, Trace?" Christine whispered.

Traci rubbed her eyes and nodded. "Yeah. It's just . . . it makes me sad to come here." For once Christine remained silent, and Traci was grateful. She needed to be strong for the coming confrontation with Corky. Unlike last time, she intended to stay put and talk to him.

Mrs. Evans emerged from the kitchen, her face lighting up when she saw Traci. "Traci! How are you, dear? How's your head?" Her brow wrinkled with concern as she inspected the slight bump on Traci's forehead.

"It's . . . it's much better, thank you." Traci rolled her eyes. "I can't *believe* I ran into your wall like an idiot."

"Nonsense," Mrs. Evans said. "It could happen to anyone. I've been meaning to replace that dark paneling and lighten up the place."

Her bright smile suddenly returned. Traci noticed that she looked happier and wondered if Mr. Evans's return had anything to do with it.

"Now that Winston's home, perhaps I can start on the remodeling. He's very good with his hands."

Traci nearly bit her tongue in two to keep from speaking her mind. Beside her, Christine began to tremble. Traci could feel it in the fingers that still gripped her arm.

"W-W-W-Win-Win—" Christine couldn't get the name out, but Mrs. Evans apparently knew what she had been trying to say.

"Yes, Winston. Corky's father."

Christine let out a blustery, relieved sigh. "Oh, *that* Winston!"

Mrs. Evans shot Christine a puzzled look. "Yes. Who did you think I meant?"

"Um, this is my friend, Christine Abernathy," Traci said hastily, hoping to change the subject before Christine said something else they'd both regret.

"Nice to meet you, Christine. Any friend of Traci's is a friend of mine."

"You . . . you too," Christine stammered.

Her friend's eyes were wide as saucers. Traci heaved an inward sigh. If meeting Corky's mother scared Christine this badly, how would she react to meeting Corky?

"So what are you two girls up to?" Mrs. Evans asked.

Traci gave a guilty start. "Oh, um, we were just wondering if you would . . . mind if we used Corky's computer. I've . . . mine is being upgraded."

"Yeah, mine, too," Christine hastily added.

Very casually, Traci nudged Christine's foot, hoping she'd get the hint. Mrs. Evans couldn't have known that Christine even *had* a computer. "We've got a paper due tomorrow—"

83

"Science project," Christine cut in. "We're working on it together."

Time for a harder nudge. Traci flopped a friendly arm around Christine's shoulders and managed to cop a painful pinch. She owed her one anyway. "We'll be so quiet you won't even know we're here."

Mrs. Evans shook her head. "You know I don't care if you use anything of Corky's." A shadow passed over her face. She lowered her voice. "Winston didn't hear about Corky's passing until a month ago. He's upset that he missed the funeral."

Again Traci had to bite her tongue. Why did the man bother coming home after Corky's death, when he hadn't bothered coming home when Corky was alive and needed him? She grabbed Christine's arm. "Come on, Christine. Let's get to work on that paper. Thanks, Mrs. Evans. We'll make sure we leave everything the way we found it."

"Don't worry, darling. Having you here is almost like having Corky around again."

You have no idea, Traci thought as she tugged Christine down the hall. When they were out of earshot, she hissed at her friend, "I thought I told you to let *me* do the talking?"

Christine yanked her arm free and shot Traci an apologetic look. "You know I talk too much when I get nervous, Trace. Give me a break, will ya?"

They stopped in front of Corky's door. Traci forcefully turned Christine around and pointed to the wall at the end of the hall. "See that wall? It doesn't move, so if you decide you want to start running, make sure you watch where you're going."

"Very funny."

"I'm not joking." She wasn't. "And don't you *dare* scream, okay? You'll upset Mrs. Evans, and that will upset Corky."

"Ooh," Christine said with a sneer. "What's he going to do, boo me to death?"

Traci decided to let that one go. She suspected Christine was bluffing, anyway. She put her hand on the doorknob. It was cold, just like the last time. "Here goes nothing," she muttered.

"You're probably more right than you think," Christine muttered back. "It probably *is* nothing."

The door swung open beneath her hand. She moved inside, aware that Christine was hugging her back instead of standing beside her. So much for not being afraid of a little booing from a ghost. "Shut the door, Christine."

"Wh-why?"

"Because he doesn't want his mother to hear him." Traci tried to hide her exasperation. Christine's obvious fear was contagious. "He won't talk until we do."

The door clicked shut.

"Thanks," Traci whispered, then let out a surprised yelp as Christine barreled into her, sending her into the middle of the room. She caught herself before she went tumbling forward. Swinging around, she glared at her friend. "What's *wrong* with you?"

Christine's face was bleached white. Her eyes were enormous. She opened her mouth, closed it, then opened it again. Finally, a squeaky whisper emerged. "I . . . I . . . didn't close the d-door." She lifted her arm and pointed a badly shaking finger just beyond Traci's shoulder. "I think . . . think . . . *he* did!"

Traci's heart froze in her chest. Was she about to see Corky in ghost form?

Slowly, she turned.

Chapter Eight

He was sitting at his computer, fading in and out like a bad hologram.

Neither girl moved a muscle. Traci didn't think she *could* move, and she didn't think Christine wanted to.

"I'm still working on the appearance thing," Corky said, sounding embarrassed. He cocked his head, trying to look around Traci to the hovering girl behind her. "I take it this is the infamous Christine?"

Traci's mouth felt as if someone had stuffed it with cotton. "Y-yes." She tried to pull Christine around so that Corky could see her, but it was like trying to remove gum from the bottom of a sneaker.

Christine wasn't budging.

"She's a little scared," Traci explained. Her face flushed. The truth was, *she* was scared, too. "We've . . . we've never seen a real ghost before."

"It's just me, Trace. Your old friend Corky." Corky flashed her a familiar, lopsided smile. "Even if I wanted to hurt you, I doubt that I could. It took me a week to figure out how to touch objects to make them move. I kept sliding right through them. You've both seen the movie *Ghost*, right? Well, that movie was more accurate than anybody could have realized." His smile disappeared in a flash. "I guess you saw . . . *him*, huh?"

Both girls nodded. Traci licked her dry lips and tried her voice again. "He looks older, but he was nice to me."

Corky's face took on the form of a thundercloud. Traci gasped; Christine let out a frightened squeak, then clamped her hand over her mouth.

His face resumed its normal, familiar lines. Once again he was just the faded image of a thirteen-year-old boy. "Sorry. Sometimes I literally wear my emotions. I've been trying to figure out how to get out of this room; so far nothing's worked."

"Oh." Traci swallowed hard, wishing Christine would unplaster herself from her back. She could feel her friend's heart pounding away. "How . . . how are you?" What was a person supposed to say to a ghost?

"Well, obviously I'm not fine," Corky said, attempting to joke. When Traci didn't smile, he sobered. "I can't believe *he* had the nerve to come back. I can't believe my mother let him in!" He made fists of his hands and struck the keyboard in front of him.

Traci jumped as the keyboard shuddered. Christine pressed even closer to her, if that were possible. "It's okay," Traci whispered to her friend. "I'd be mad, too."

"What if he hurts us?" Christine whispered, digging her fingers into Traci's back.

"He won't. He can't." Traci wasn't afraid of Corky hurting them; she was just afraid. Louder, she said, "Corky, maybe your father's changed."

Corky snorted, glaring at her as if she were the enemy. "I can't believe you! I don't care if he *has* changed. He left us, and he has no business coming

89

back. Mom was fine without him."

"Was she?" Traci relaxed a fraction. The more she listened to him, the more he sounded like plain old Corky. Not a ghost, but a little boy who'd been badly hurt over his father's desertion. Taking a deep breath, she plunged ahead. "I think she was incredibly lonely, especially after you . . . " She swallowed hard, unable to speak the words. "She lives by herself, Corky. She has no friends, doesn't go anywhere but to work. She needs somebody."

"Not him!" Corky shouted. He floated from the chair, flashing in and out like a Christmas bulb.

It was too much for Christine. She dug her claws into the shirt on Traci's back and yanked her backward until they both slammed into the door.

The three of them froze, listening to see if Mr. or Mrs. Evans had heard the commotion.

When neither of them came to investigate, Traci relaxed. She yanked her shirt out of Christine's death grip and turned around, grabbing Christine's shoulders. She gave her a little shake, trying to sound firm when her own insides were quaking. "If you can't handle it, then get out. You're going to blow Corky's cover."

"You . . . you . . . you . . . " Christine looked wild-eyed and near hysteria. "He's . . . he's . . . he's . . . "

More gently, Traci said, "Go on, Christine. Wait for me out in the hall. I won't be mad at you."

Christine shook her head wildly. "Not . . . not without you."

Forcing a smile, Traci said, "What, you think he's going to eat my soul or something?"

Behind them, Corky started making gross smacking sounds.

Traci glared at him over her shoulder. "Shut up, Corky! Can't you see she's terrified?"

"Sorry."

Just like old times, Corky didn't sound the least bit sorry. The realization helped Traci to relax even further. She concentrated on her friend again. She was beginning to grow worried about her sanity. She didn't think they'd invented the saying "scared to death" for nothing. "Christine, Corky won't hurt us. He's just a thirteen-year-old punk ghost—"

"Hey! I resent that statement!"

"Shut up, Corky." To Christine, she said, "If it helps, think of him like you would think of one of your bratty brothers."

"Hey!"

"Put a cork in it, Corky!" Traci couldn't believe she and Corky had slipped into their old bickering routine as if two years hadn't gone by.

As if he weren't a ghost.

She shook the thought away before it spooked her too badly. If she lost it, there would be no hope for Christine. "Are you going to be okay? If you want to leave, then I'll go with you."

"Hey!" Corky protested. "That's not fair! What about me? I was your friend first! Just because she's a wimp—"

Christine startled them both by saying, "I'm not a wimp, you obnoxious cloud of smoke." Fire had replaced the terror in her eyes. She pushed Traci aside and stomped up to Corky.

Traci felt as if someone could have knocked her over with a feather, she was so amazed at her friend's sudden transformation.

Jabbing a finger at his flickering form, Christine continued to rip him apart. "*You* might have been her friend first, but now *I'm* her best friend, so you might as well get used to it!"

Traci smothered a laugh at Corky's stunned expression. When Christine got riled, she could be really intimidating.

"You can't just come back from the dead and take over, Corky. We're older and wiser than you, so you'd best get used to it." She folded her arms and glared at him. "And if you try to scare us again with those evil faces, I'm going to punch your . . . your . . . " She paused a heartbeat, then resumed, "I'm going to knock you into the next world myself!"

Corky threw up his hands in a gesture of surrender. He was grinning. "Hey, I'm cool with that. No more scary faces."

His grin slipped a notch, revealing a vulnerability that tugged at Traci's heartstrings. She didn't think Christine was immune, either.

"Just don't leave, okay?" he pleaded.

Christine snorted, but Traci caught her mellowed expression as she turned away from Corky, and knew that Corky had won her over.

"I'll stay," she told Traci. "I think Corky and I understand each other." She rolled her eyes. "And you're right; he reminds me of my rotten brothers with that smart mouth."

Traci let out a smothered shriek as Christine flopped back onto Corky's bed, scattering his foggy form into oblivion.

"What? What is it?" Christine demanded, unaware of what she'd done.

The air behind her crackled. Tiny lights flickered, then came slowly together until Corky took on human form again. He looked exasperated.

"If you knew how much work that was . . . " He shook his head ruefully, glancing at Traci, who had covered her mouth with her hand. "Where did you find her, anyway?"

Now that Christine was no longer afraid, there was no stopping her. She began to tell Corky how they met as if he was the boy next door, instead of a ghost who couldn't hold his shape.

Traci slowly approached the bed and sat beside Christine.

It really was Corky, she thought, aching to reach out and touch him.

"That's the fifth time Brad's had to stop and tie his shoelaces," Traci said to Christine. She gave her bottom lip a worried nibble. She and Christine were sitting in the bleachers watching the Friday-night football game, surrounded by most of their classmates and quite a few parents. Their team, the Beachmont Wildcats, were having to work hard to stay ahead of their rival team, the Kramerville Indians.

"That's about as many times as he had to adjust his helmet," Christine said. "See? There he goes again."

Traci frowned as she watched Brad pause to adjust his helmet, then bend down and tie his shoelace for the sixth time. "What's wrong, I wonder?"

"Mom would say he's got ants in his pants."

"My mother would say it's a nervous habit, but I've never noticed him doing it before."

They held their breath as the Wildcats gathered at the end of the field for a kickoff. The Indians now had the ball. Brad was number twenty-two and easy to spot as he bent over.

Suddenly he straightened and grabbed the sides of his white skintight pants.

"What's he doing now?" Christine asked.

"I don't know." Traci craned her neck to see over the tall guy sitting in front of her. "It looks like . . . he's holding up his pants."

"What the heck?"

"That's what it looks like, but those pants are skintight, so it's not likely they'd be falling down."

Christine giggled. "He sure is acting weird tonight. Maybe that last tackle was worse than we thought. Maybe he's suffering from a head injury."

"Or maybe there are invisible gremlins out on the field, running around untying shoes and . . ." Traci froze with her mouth open. She turned to look at Christine as Christine turned to look at her. Their openmouthed expressions were identical.

"Corky!" they shrieked simultaneously.

Traci ground her teeth. "If we're right, I'm going to kill him!"

"He's already dead, Trace," Christine pointed out dryly.

"Then I'm going to make him *wish* he were dead."

Christine gasped, then jumped to her feet. "Hey!" she cried, swinging around and glaring at the guy sitting behind her. "You'd better—"

Before she could finish her sentence, Traci yanked her back down, throwing the poor guy an apologetic look. She pulled Christine close and whispered fiercely, "What are you doing?"

"Someone unhooked my bra!" Christine whispered just as fiercely. She continued to glare at the guy behind her.

"You idiot! *He* didn't do it!"

Realization dawned on Christine's face. She looked carefully around her, then back to Traci. "Where is he?"

"I don't know, but I know he's here." She smiled grimly. "He's been tormenting Brad throughout the game." Louder, for Corky's benefit, she said, "And he'd better stop messing with Brad *right now*."

"Yeah," Christine added, sounding peeved, "And me, too. That's sexual harassment."

Traci knew the moment he settled his invisible form between them. She could feel his cold shoulder pressing against hers.

"What are you going to do, sue me?" he asked Christine in a normal voice.

In a panic, Traci glanced at the guy behind them, relieved to find his attention on the game.

Where *hers* should be.

Staring straight ahead, she said, "You should be ashamed of yourself, tormenting Brad that way. He's playing football!"

Corky snickered. "He's trying, anyway. Kinda hard to do when you have to keep stopping to tie your shoes."

"So you admit it." Traci wished she could kick him, but she knew he probably wouldn't feel it.

"And if you touch me again," Christine warned, "I'm going to get Mom's Dustbuster and suck you into it, then plug it up with a pair of my little brother's dirty underwear."

"Ooh, I'm so scared."

"You'd better be, freak."

"Hey, that was uncalled for!" Corky managed to sound wounded and amused at the same time. "I don't think I'd put *ghost* and *freak* in the same category, Miss thirty-two triple A cup."

Christine gasped.

Traci groaned.

"You . . . you . . . " Christine was obviously too furious to stay seated—and keep her voice down. "You *looked* at my bra size?" she shouted.

Traci put her hands over her face. She knew better than anyone how sensitive Christine was about her small chest. It really wasn't that small, and they both knew she still had some growing to do, but in the meantime . . .

"You . . . you . . . " Insults didn't satisfy Christine. Besides, she could barely be heard above the sound of Corky laughing. With a howl of rage, she made a fist and swung at the air between them.

Her fist went straight through.

Then around.

And into the face of the unsuspecting guy sitting behind them.

Chapter Nine

"I'm never going to be able to show my face at a football game again," Christine said darkly. Her gaze darted constantly around them, searching for any sign of Corky. "You just wait until I get my hands on him."

"That's the problem," Traci said, hoping to defuse Christine's justified anger. "You *can't* get your hands on him. He's a ghost, remember?"

"A holy terror, you mean. He's worse than my brothers, and believe me when I say I never thought I'd be uttering *those* words!"

"He didn't mean any harm."

"The heck he didn't! Do you know who I slugged in the mouth?" She didn't give Traci time to answer. "Dustin Hall's dad! You remember Dustin Hall? The same hot guy I've had a crush on for two years?" Christine groaned and covered her face as if she couldn't face the thought. She spoke between her fingers. "Has he always been this . . . this *mean?*"

No doubt whom she was talking about. Traci felt compelled to defend her old friend. "Mischievous."

"That's not the word I'd use. I say he's a mean, selfish, freaky little—"

"Shh! Here comes Brad." Traci's heartbeat doubled, then tripled as Brad made his way over to them from the locker room. His hair was damp from his shower, and he looked muscled and fit in his jeans and hunter-green pullover fleece shirt.

She swallowed hard and gave him a bright smile,

elbowing Christine just for good measure. If Christine said one single word about their ghostly friend, she was going to lock them together in Corky's bedroom and throw away the key. She didn't think Corky had figured out how to go through walls yet.

"Great game, Brad!" Traci said the moment he reached them. She had to hold her own hands to keep from throwing them around his hunky neck. Man, was he buff! From the top of his tousled blond head to the bottom of his size thirteen feet.

To her intense pleasure, he slipped his arm around her waist as if they'd been a couple for ages. He smiled down at her, and her mouth went dry. She knew she was gazing up at him like a lovesick puppy, but she honestly couldn't stop.

His smile faded a bit. His voice was deep and slightly embarrassed-sounding as he said, "Thanks, Traci, but I know I didn't play very well tonight. For some reason I couldn't keep it together."

From the corner of her eye, Traci saw Christine subtly adjust her twisted bra. Traci had tried to fasten it through her shirt behind the bleachers after the game and had only partially succeeded.

Christine caught her warning look, but was too miffed to ignore it. She crossed her arms over her chest and muttered, "I know exactly how you feel."

Brad tilted his head in her direction. "You say something, Christine?"

"Um, she said you looked good on the field." Traci stared pointedly at Christine. "Didn't you, Christine?" Christine fumed for a moment, then heaved a long-suffering sigh.

"Sure. Yeah, that's what I said." The moment Brad looked away, Christine rolled her eyes. "You sure you don't mind giving me a ride home, Brad?"

"Of course not."

He put his arm around Traci's shoulders and began walking toward the parking lot. Christine followed.

Traci could hardly contain her happiness. She couldn't believe she was walking beside Brad, on their way to his car to go out on a date! Part of her felt guilty, however, that Christine didn't have a guy of her own, but she knew that it was just a matter of time before some gorgeous guy noticed her friend. Christine was very pretty, with her straight black hair and dark chocolate eyes.

As they made their way to Brad's car, she got lost in a daydream where she and Brad and Christine and someone like Dustin Hall—who really was a hunk—were out together on a double date. They would have so much fun—

"Man, I don't believe it!"

Brad's agitated exclamation jarred Traci out of her beautiful daydream. She blinked and followed his gaze to the black Jeep parked on the grass.

"A flat tire." Traci shivered as Brad dropped his arm

and hunkered down by the tire. Christine came to stand beside her. Traci knew without looking that her friend was wearing a smug expression. "Don't say it," she whispered. "I know you're thinking it, but don't say it."

"Well," Brad said with a sigh as he straightened and shot her a puzzled, sheepish grin. "I guess I'll just have to change it."

Traci waited, hardly breathing, as Brad moved to the hatch and unlocked it. He pulled out the doughnut tire and bounced it on the ground.

It didn't bounce back.

She closed her eyes and said beneath her breath, "I'm going to kill Corky."

Christine didn't hesitate. "He doesn't mean any harm, remember? And besides, you can't kill him. He's already dead."

Sometimes, Traci thought, choking on a furious scream, her friend could be such a pain in the butt!

"Christine's dad didn't look too happy about having to come get her," Brad observed.

They were leaning against his Jeep waiting on *his* dad to arrive and take them to the nearest station to pump up the spare tire. Traci had managed to convince Brad the air had gone out from disuse. Corky was mischievous, but she couldn't believe he'd actually damage the tires.

She hoped she was right.

"Her dad watches *Larry King Live*, and woe to anyone who gets in his way," Traci explained. "The condition of her getting to come with me tonight was that she have her own ride home."

"What about her mom? Doesn't she drive?"

"Yeah, but *she* takes a long leisurely bath while *he* watches *Larry King Live*." She rolled her eyes to emphasize her next statement. "Mom says they're in a rut, but I think she's just jealous."

Brad nodded. "Yeah, at least Christine's parents know how to keep it together."

They fell silent after that for a few moments. Traci knew he was thinking about his parents, and hated that she'd dug up that old ghost.

Oops. Bad analogy, but speaking of ghosts . . . Traci wondered as she'd been wondering for the past half hour if Corky were still lurking around. The thought made her uncomfortable. She loved Corky, but the prospect of him spying on her with Brad made her jumpy. They were going to have to have a long, serious talk very soon.

"There's Dad."

Traci stiffened, watching the approaching headlights. She was about to meet the macho man who had called her mom ditzy. What if she hated him on sight? What if he said something about her mom and she couldn't keep her mouth shut?

"Come on, Traci," Brad said, apparently sensing her tension. "He won't eat you."

He might try, Traci thought, if his dad knew she was the spawn of the redheaded devil who had rammed into his BMW. Reluctantly, she let go of Brad's hand so that he could throw the flat spare in his dad's trunk. The moment he was finished, he returned and took her hand again. He began to tug her toward the idling car.

Ted Davidson rolled down his window, grinning at them. "A flat tire, huh?" He was staring at Traci as he added, "I tried to pull that once, but her parents didn't go for it. They grounded her for a month for being late."

Brad gave her hand an encouraging squeeze. "Luckily, I'm not lying, and she's not late." He shot Traci a warm smile that went straight down to her toes. "Dad, this is Traci. Traci, this is Ted."

"Hi, Mr. Davidson." Traci waved at him, then felt dumb for doing it. Thank God it was dark and he couldn't see her blushing!

"Brad, you didn't tell me how beautiful she was," Ted teased.

I can't like him, Traci reminded herself. He was the enemy. He'd called her mother ditzy, and was probably going to sue the pants off her. They'd have to sell the house and move into a trailer park. She'd have to wear hand-me-downs and eat peanut butter and crackers twenty-four-seven—

"Traci?"

She blinked at Brad. "Huh?"

"Where did you go off to? Dad was asking you if you'd like to eat dinner with us tomorrow night. He makes a mean lasagna."

She loved lasagna. But no, she couldn't. "Um, I—"

"Bring your mom along, too," Ted said. His smile was warm and friendly. "But I warn you, if she looks anything like her daughter, I might have to ask her out on a date."

There was a definite snicker from somewhere behind her.

Traci choked, then turned it into a cough. Brad patted her on the back.

"You okay?"

"Um, yeah, yeah. Just swallowed wrong or something." Her face was on fire. She no longer had to ask herself if Corky was around. Hastily she said, "Maybe we should get out of here if we're going for pizza. I have to be home by midnight."

She literally pushed Brad into the backseat of the BMW when he opened the door. Quickly she climbed in behind him and slammed the door, then locked it. Could Corky come through the car door? Was he already inside?

When she turned to Brad, she found him watching her, wearing an understandably bemused expression.

"If I didn't know better, I'd think someone was after you." He laughed to show he was joking, but the suspicion in his eyes lingered.

Traci felt like kicking herself. Brad was no dumb jock, and her actions would look strange to *anyone* watching. Her face heated another five degrees. "It's a habit," she lied. To her relief, Ted put the car into gear and headed out of the parking lot.

"Sorry about the car," he said, glancing at her in the rearview mirror. "I was in an accident earlier this week. Did Brad tell you?"

"I told her, Dad." Brad shook his head and sighed, mouthing, *Here it goes*, to Traci.

He knew his dad well, Traci discovered.

"She rammed right into the passenger side of the car. Said she'd dropped her nail file. Can you believe that?"

This time Ted shook his head, and Traci couldn't help but note the resemblance between father and son. She hoped that wasn't a bad sign.

"I think she was actually a blonde instead of a redhead."

"Dad!"

It was the first time Traci had seen Brad anything but cheerful and friendly—other than puzzled, that is. Now he sounded mad.

"What?" Ted grinned at Traci in the mirror. "She knows I'm joking, don't you, hon?"

Not wanting to insult Brad's father, Traci nodded. But she kept her lips tightly sealed. Every instinct in her cried out to stick up for her mom, but in doing so she'd have to own up to being her daughter, and she wasn't quite ready for that.

"You're being a jerk," Brad said in a scolding voice that made Traci's lips twitch.

Ted turned on his blinker just seconds before he gunned the BMW and cut in front of a fast-moving vehicle coming from the opposite direction.

Traci heard the squeal of brakes from the car behind them, and the harsh blaring of the irate driver Ted had leaped in front of. She slammed her eyelids shut. She did not want to think about how close they had come to getting creamed.

"Told you," Brad whispered in her ear, his breath warm and tickling.

And just like that, she melted. She couldn't wait to get him alone. She couldn't wait for that first kiss. It would be the absolute best kiss, she just *knew* it, one that she would remember for the rest of her life.

A life she was already dreaming of spending with Brad. They could be high school sweethearts, like Christine's mom and dad.

They came to a neck-snapping stop alongside the air pump. Brad nuzzled her cheek with his lips before opening the car door.

"I'll be right back," he told her.

Ted shut off the engine and opened his door, as well. "I'll go inside and see if I can borrow an air gauge. You don't want to put too much air in one of those wimpy tires."

Traci was anticipating a moment alone to catch her breath. She watched as Ted slid from the driver's seat and stood beside the car.

He had taken a few steps away from the car when the engine started up again. "What the . . . " He frowned through the car window at the ignition.

"What is it, Dad?"

With a dreadful feeling in her bones, Traci watched as Ted opened the car door and reached across the steering wheel to turn the key again. When he cast her a half-suspicious, puzzled glance, she gave him a weak, innocent smile.

"Must be a short in the ignition," Ted muttered, slamming the door again.

The moment the door closed, the engine started again.

Traci groaned and lowered her head. She began to bang it against the seat.

"What's going on?" Brad asked again, coming over to look for himself.

Ted jerked the door open and stared first at Traci— who was obviously too far away to turn the key— then at the ignition key. "It's the darnedest thing! I've never seen a car turn itself on like that!" After a few moments of frowning silence, he shrugged and left it running, closing the car door.

Traci jumped as someone or something touched her cheek. It didn't take her long to figure out who.

"He shouldn't have said that about your mother," Corky whispered in a righteous tone.

Traci didn't bother looking for him. She was afraid the sight of him would provoke a physical attack. "How did you know he was talking about my mother?"

"Hm. Let me see. Because you looked mad as heck. Because he said the woman had broken a nail. Because I was at your house before I came to the game and your mother was on the phone to your aunt Gillian, talking about the accident."

Evenly, Traci said, "If you don't leave us alone, I'm never going to speak to you again, Corky. I mean it." She'd left her cell phone at home, but obviously the wise move had been in vain.

"Fine, but there's one little problem with that request."

She stifled a sigh. "What?"

"I haven't figured out how to fly around or just appear. I walked to your house; then I walked to the game, so I need a ride home. I'm pretty tired."

Understandably, she felt no sympathy. "You left out the part where you followed Brad around on the field and tormented him, and you left out the part where you raced to his Jeep and let the air out of his tires. I guess all that activity would make anyone tired, even a ghost."

"I'm so glad you understand, Trace."

Before Traci could respond, the car door opened. Brad stuck his head inside and looked around, then focused on her.

"Who are you talking to?"

Traci's smile felt about as phony as the *National Enquirer*. "Myself. I was talking to myself."

Chapter Ten

"Now that we're finally here, I don't want to go in," Brad said as he killed the engine and slid his arm along the car seat.

They had made it to the pizza joint after stopping at the corner of her street so that she could look for the lipstick she claimed she'd dropped while waiting for him. She hadn't really lost it, of course, but she wanted Corky out of that car and lying seemed the only way. She couldn't very well ask Brad to give her ghost friend a ride home.

Traci looked around the parking lot of Charlie's, recognizing a few cars. The place was packed, as usual, especially after a football game.

She was torn. She wanted to be alone with Brad, but she also wanted to be *seen* with Brad. She got an idea. "Hey, why don't we go inside and order a pizza to go? Then we could park somewhere and have a picnic in the Jeep."

Brad's expression lit up. "That's a great idea, Traci." He brushed his fingertips against her cheek, lowering his impossibly long eyelashes. "Smart *and* beautiful. Wow. How lucky can a guy get? Come on. I want to show you off."

Great minds think alike, Traci thought happily as she followed him from the Jeep. They laced fingers on the way into the pizza place, making her feel extra special.

"Hey, Traci!" Tabitha Sweeny, a casual friend of Traci's, waved at her from a booth in the corner as they made their way through the crowd to the counter.

Traci waved back, basking in the glow of several envious stares. Julia Frank sat in the booth with Tabitha, and Traci waved at her, too. Once upon a time the four of them, counting Christine, had been inseparable, but too much bickering had driven them apart. Eventually she had paired with Christine and Tabitha had paired with Julia. Sometimes she missed having them around. Maybe she'd invite them to the Halloween party.

Oh, man. The party! She couldn't invite Brad, not after his father had a run-in—literally—with her mother! She didn't want Brad to know. She didn't want her *mom* to know who Brad's father was.

What a mess.

Warm, strong fingers cupped her chin and turned her face in his direction. She gulped as Brad's green gaze swept over her features. The appreciative look in his eyes made her knees wobbly.

The noise around them seemed to fade.

"If it wasn't for being with you," he said softly, "I'd say this night pretty much sucks."

She licked her lips, unable to look away. "You . . . you won the game."

His smile was rueful. "You mean my *teammates* won the game. I was too busy tying my shoelaces to do much. Then the flat tires . . . I'm beginning to think

I've gotten on the wrong side of a ghost."

Traci swallowed very, very softly. She could feel her eyes widening in shock, and tried to stop it. "A . . . a ghost? You believe in ghosts?"

Before he could answer, the guy standing next to him at the counter slapped him on the back, knocking him into Traci.

"Hey, man! Saw the game tonight. Didn't your mama teach you how to tie your shoes?"

Several of the guys surrounding them laughed. Traci stiffened, wondering how Brad was going to handle their good-natured ribbing. Would he get mad? Start a fight? Or would he just walk away?

Turned out she was wrong all the way around. Brad twisted around, grinning at Mitch McNew. Traci recognized him from her English class.

"Hey, McNew." Brad laughed with them, not looking the least bit mad. Sheepish, yes, and a little red in the face, but not mad. "I don't know what happened, but I do know I'm going to get some new shoelaces."

"And some new pants!" someone called out from the crowd. More laughter followed.

Traci realized they were fast becoming the center of attention. So far Brad had been a good sport about the teasing, but how much could a guy take? She was really going to tell Corky off for putting Brad through this! Couldn't Corky see that Brad was a great guy?

She caught the waitress's eye and waved her over.

"Sandy, is our pizza ready? We're in a hurry."

Sandy, whom she knew from school, said she'd check. She disappeared through the kitchen door, then emerged with a boxed pizza. She slapped it on the counter. "That'll be thirteen dollars and twenty-seven cents."

Brad handed her fifteen and told her to keep the change. They made it to the door before their path was blocked by Adam Luke, the one and only guy Traci had seriously dated before Brad.

Their brief relationship hadn't exactly ended on good terms.

Traci braced herself, wishing she had warned Brad about Adam. "Adam. What do you want?" She wasn't about to waste her breath on amenities, and she wasn't going to pretend she liked him.

Adam smiled, but the smile didn't quite reach his eyes. "Just wanted to say hi."

"Hi," Traci said curtly. "And good-bye." She grabbed Brad's arm and tried to pull him toward the door. If she had to plow through Adam to get there, then so be it.

Adam held his ground and, to her frustration, so did Brad.

"Hey, hold up," Adam said. "I just wanted to chat with our star quarterback a moment."

Glaring at Adam probably wouldn't work, but Traci tried it anyway. "You don't know him, and he doesn't know you. Would you mind letting us pass?" She ground her teeth as Brad thrust out a friendly hand, apparently oblivious to the tension between them.

"Hey, man. I'm Brad Davidson. I think I've seen you around."

They shook hands. Traci didn't like the gleam in Adam's eye, and she soon found out why.

"Yeah, I've seen you around, too. So, have you met Traci's mom yet? She's one hot babe!"

If they hadn't been touching shoulders, Traci might have missed the way Brad stiffened.

"No, I haven't, but when I do, I'll have more respect for her than you apparently do." All this said with the same steady voice Brad always used. "Now I know why Traci dumped you."

Traci was speechless as Brad moved forward, forcing the disconcerted Adam to move aside. She followed him to the Jeep without looking back.

Once inside, she managed to unlock her vocal cords. "Thanks for sticking up for my mom. How did you know about me and Adam?"

Brad didn't answer right away. He carefully placed the pizza box on the backseat, then started the Jeep and backed out of the parking lot. When they were on the road again, he glanced at her.

He was still smiling, but his eyes had darkened, the only evidence of his lingering anger.

"You're welcome, and I heard the rumors."

Heat crept into Traci's face. She couldn't look at him, afraid she'd read censure in his eyes. "Um, that's why I stopped dating him. He . . . he was spreading rumors about me, and they weren't true."

"I never thought they were," Brad said softly. "I knew he was a creep before I met him. Laura told me."

"Laura?" Jealousy speared through her. Who was Laura? And what was she to Brad?

"Yeah, Laura Eubanks. Know her? She's a friend of mine."

Knowing who she was didn't lessen Traci's jealousy. Laura Eubanks was nice. She was also very popular with the boys, a cheerleader, and last year's homecoming queen. She had long blond hair, vivid blue eyes, a heart-shaped face, and legs that would have made her mother—who had great legs—envious.

But she was *nice. Darn it.* "Yeah, I know her. She's cool." *And she'd better keep her long, immaculate claws to herself,* Traci thought, surprised at the uncharacteristically hostile thought. She should be ashamed of herself, in light of the fact that Laura had set Brad straight about the rumors Adam had spread.

They parked in a well-lit area next to the high school to eat the pizza. Traci was relieved. A tiny part of her had been afraid Brad would suddenly shed his sheep's clothing and drive up to Widow's Point.

Her expression must have been obvious.

"You still don't trust me, do you, Traci?"

117

She jerked, nearly dumping her pizza onto her lap. She scrambled to catch it, getting pizza sauce on her fingers in the process.

Brad handed her a napkin, laughing at her.

She found herself smiling along with him. "I'm sorry. I guess dating a guy like Adam has made me a little suspicious."

"You don't have to be," he said seriously.

"I know." She *did* know. She just hadn't convinced the saner side of her brain yet. "It isn't fair that you should have to suffer for Adam's sins."

"Adam's sins. Hm."

They both burst out laughing.

"Don't worry," Brad said, "I don't feel like I'm suffering." His voice dropped an octave, kicking her heart into overdrive. "In fact, I'm having a great time. How about you?"

She happily nodded, licking pizza sauce from her lips. Her friends claimed they couldn't eat around boys, but Traci felt completely relaxed around Brad.

Well, with the exception of an irregular heartbeat, sweaty palms, and weak knees.

"Wait, you've got pizza sauce on your mouth."

She held her breath as Brad leaned forward and kissed the corner of her mouth. She felt the warm wetness of his tongue as he licked the pizza sauce from her skin. With anyone else, she was certain she would have thought the action gross.

With Brad, it was exhilarating.

He lifted his head and opened his eyes. They looked soft and dreamy, just as she suspected *hers* looked.

"I've had enough pizza," he said huskily. "How about you?"

"Hm." She gave him her uneaten pizza slice, her entire body trembling with anticipation as she watched him return it to the pizza box along with his own.

Then he came back to her, slowly lowering his mouth onto hers. Gently, sweetly, he kissed her. Traci put her arm around his neck and deepened the kiss.

She jumped as he traced her closed lips with his tongue, then tentatively opened them. Taking his time. Allowing her to either resist or comply.

Traci complied, experiencing her first French kiss with Brad Davidson. The feel of his tongue against hers made her heart leap inside her chest.

It was wild. It was exciting. It was—

"*Psst.* Traci! Out here."

Brad jerked back, his pupils dilating with alarm. "Did you hear that?"

"What? No, no. I didn't hear anything." Over Brad's shoulder, Traci saw Corky waving madly through the Jeep window, his ghostly form flickering like a bad connection. She stifled a gasp. "I, um, I think I need to get some air."

"Are you okay? Did I do something to upset you?"

His obvious concern made her feel awful—and furious at Corky. "No, no! I think maybe . . . maybe it was the pizza. I'll just be a minute."

He looked agonized, as if he'd done something wrong. Traci ground her teeth and vowed to make a certain ghost pay for this. She scrambled out of the Jeep and slammed the door, leaning against it. She folded her arms and waited, too mad to speak. Corky wasted no time coming around the Jeep to her side. She was thankful, he'd made himself invisible. "Sorry about this, Trace, but I didn't know who else to turn to."

Her back was to the Jeep. Nevertheless, she barely moved her lips as she whispered furiously, "What is it *now*, Corky? And couldn't this wait until I got home?"

"No, it couldn't," Corky said gravely. "That . . . that *man* is trying to talk Mom into selling the house and moving away. He says he wants to start over in another town, but I think he's trying to rip her off!"

Chapter Eleven

She needed some time alone to think about that kiss, the upcoming party, Susan and Ted doing the road tango, and Corky's problems.

"We've got to do something, Trace. We can't just let that man run over Mom and take her for everything she has."

But unfortunately Corky wouldn't leave her room long enough for her to catch her breath. She was lying facedown on her bed, wishing he'd disappear so that she could relive that incredible kiss. "That man is your father, Corky. It's not like he's a stranger off the street."

"Yes," Corky shrieked, earning a warning look from Traci. He prudently lowered his voice. "He *is* a stranger as far as I'm concerned, and he's not going to get away with ripping Mom off!"

Traci turned to her side so that she faced Corky, who had taken a seat at her computer. "What if he's not trying to rip her off? What if he simply wants to make up for everything he's done?"

Corky glowered. "He could never make up for leaving us."

A knock at the door startled them. Corky granted her silent wish and disappeared with an audible popping noise.

"Traci? Are you still awake?"

It was after midnight. Wasn't everyone awake at this hour? With a long-suffering sigh, she rose and went to the door. Maybe if she blocked the doorway, her mom would get the hint. She opened the door to find Susan standing there in a short nightie that would have been better suited—in Traci's opinion—to someone her own age.

"I'm still awake." She didn't have to struggle to sound groggy. She *was* groggy.

Susan's brow puckered. She slanted Traci a suspicious look. "I could have sworn I heard you talking to someone." She peered around Traci, her gaze sweeping the empty room. "You don't have a boy in here, do you?"

"Very funny, Mom." Since she considered Corky a brat instead of a boy, she didn't feel as if she were lying.

"Hm. Well, I was about to go to bed when I realized I didn't get to meet Brad. How come you didn't bring him in? You know how I like to—"

"I told you, he had two flat tires at the game and we were running late. He said he'll come inside next time."

"Did you have a good time?"

Despite Corky's interference and the ugly incident at the pizza place, Traci was able to say with total honesty, "I had a *great* time."

"Are you going to invite him to the party? Because if you are, I need to add him to the list. I'm sending out the invitations tomorrow."

"Um . . . " *Think fast, Trace!* "No, he won't be able to make it."

"Why not?"

"Well, because . . . " Behind her, Corky snickered. Traci hastily tried to cover the sound with a cough. "He's going to be out of town with his dad." She hated lying. When she lied, her face turned pink. Most of the time Susan picked up on that signal.

Thank goodness this wasn't one of those times. Maybe because she suspected she'd looked a little flushed to begin with. A date with Brad Davidson could do that to a girl.

Susan looked disappointed. "That's too bad, because I was thinking about asking his dad, too."

Not in this lifetime, Traci thought, keeping her mouth firmly shut. *Don't provide information unless asked.* She'd heard that somewhere on television. And how did Susan know Brad's father was single? Hm . . . Not something she wanted to find out at the moment, not with Corky lurking behind her, gleefully eavesdropping.

"Can we talk about the party tomorrow?" Traci asked, hiding her impatience with extreme effort.

"I suppose, pumpkin." Her mother rubbed her temple as if her head ached, prompting a pang of guilt in Traci.

"Is your head still bothering you?"

"Just a little headache." She hesitated. "The strangest

thing happened today. I was on the phone with your aunt Gillian, and I felt someone was breathing on my neck. I mean, I could actually *feel* their breath." She laughed, then winced. "Maybe that bump did more damage than I thought."

Impulsively, Traci hugged her mother. "Good night, Mom. Take care of yourself, okay?"

"I will, sweetie. You, too. Want waffles in the morning?"

"Sounds great."

"Okay, then. I love you."

"Love you, too."

The moment the door shut, Corky started making the sound of a mournful violin.

Traci glared at him. "Very funny, and what's with scaring my mom? Did you come back just so you could make everyone think they were going crazy? You remind me of that cheesy movie with Kevin Bacon, *Hollow Man*. Slipping around, scaring everyone."

"Oh, you wound me, Trace. I was just having a little fun."

"Well, do me a favor and leave Mom out of it. She had enough of your pranks when you were—" Traci bit her lip. She'd been about to say, "when you were alive," before she realized how insensitive she would sound. "I hope you aren't terrorizing your mother the way you're terrorizing everyone else."

"Nah, I wouldn't do that. But there was an incident—"

When he broke off, Traci prompted. "And? Come

on, you've been eavesdropping on me all night. I think you owe me one, or two or three."

"Well, just don't make a big deal out of it, okay? It was after you dropped me off at the corner—you stepped on my big toe, by the way."

Traci bared her teeth in a gleeful grin. "Sorry. Go ahead."

"When I got to my room, *he* was there." Corky looked uncomfortable, sparking Traci's curiosity. "He was kneeling by my bed, crying like a baby." Corky attempted a sneer, but fell short of the mark.

"What did you do?"

"I did what any self-respecting ghost would do."

"And what's that?"

"I gave him a wedgie."

"You didn't!" Traci covered her mouth to stifle her laughter. She knew she shouldn't encourage Corky. She was about to scold him when she was hit with a brilliant idea. "Corky . . . what did your dad do when you gave him a wedgie?"

"He's *not* my dad."

"Whatever."

"He's not." Corky glared at her for a moment before adding reluctantly, "The dumb man actually called out my name, as if he *knew* I was in the room."

Traci gasped. "Really?"

"Yeah. Freaked me out. Man, was I tempted to tell him off right then and there, and I would have if . . .

if it wasn't for Mom." Corky looked so sad at that moment that Traci wanted to cry. "I just don't want him upsetting her by telling her he talked to me."

"I've got an idea!"

Corky perked up. "Yeah?"

"Yeah. Make a list of all the questions you would like to ask him, if you weren't . . . if you could . . . "

"I get the picture."

"And I'll figure out a way me and Christine can get him alone and ask them *for* you."

"And I can be there?"

"No." Traci was firm on this. "I think that would be a bad idea. You might shoot off at the mouth and give the man a heart attack."

"But I don't see why I can't be there," Corky whined, sounding exactly like an overly tired thirteen-year-old. "If he can believe I exist, then why can't I let him see me?"

Traci crossed her arms over her chest. "Do you remember what happened to me when I first saw you?"

Corky nodded.

"And don't forget Christine's reaction. I've still got nail marks on my back where she tried to claw me to death."

"Oh, yeah." Corky hung his head. "I guess you're right. Okay, that sounds like a good plan. I'll just start making my list—"

"Let me rephrase that, Corky. Go *home* and make your list. And get some sleep. You look like de—Um . . . you look tired."

He moved past her to the door, pausing to put his hand on her shoulder. She felt the pressure and was oddly moved by it. Oh, how she had missed him! Blinking back tears, she shrugged his hand away, determined not to care too much this time around. He'd have to leave someday, and she didn't want to go through *that* again. Losing him the first time had left a big hole in her heart.

She thought she'd gotten over it—until she saw him again.

"Thanks, Bobcat. I knew I could count on you. Brad doesn't deserve you, you know."

"Don't start, Corky. That's another subject you and I need to talk about. Just not tonight. I'm beat."

"I guess all that kissing—"

"Corky!"

"I'm going, I'm going. Sheesh."

Then he was gone, and Traci immediately felt a sharp sense of loss. "No," she said out loud. "You can't go there again, Traci. He's not staying."

She jumped as Corky's arms slid around her waist from behind. He kissed her on the cheek, his lips as cold as the doorknob on his bedroom door.

His voice was strangely deep as he said near her ear, "I still love you, Traci. I always will."

Tears burned her throat. "I love you, too." Only she knew it wasn't the same. She was fifteen; he was still thirteen. He was a ghost.

And then there was Brad.

She was having a wonderful dream about Brad. Well, it was a *strange* dream, but wonderful anyway because Brad was in it. They were sitting smack-dab in the middle of a giant, gooey pepperoni pizza, kissing. Each time she tried to raise her hand to cup his face, she realized it was covered with gooey, stringy mozzarella cheese.

"Traci! Wake up!"

Corky's urgent voice penetrated through her subconscious. She tried to open her eyes, but they were too heavy. "Leave me alone," she mumbled, waving him away.

"I can't. I came by to give you my list."

She managed to open one eye, searching for her alarm clock on the nightstand. It was nine o'clock. She usually slept until ten on Saturdays. Had Corky forgotten? "You couldn't wait one more hour?"

"Well, *I* could have, but I thought you might want to know that your mother invited some people over for breakfast. She's going to surprise you."

"So?" What was the big deal? She'd eaten breakfast with her aunt before. Plenty of times, and so had

Corky. And if he was talking about Christine, well, that was fine, too. In fact, her mom had plenty of friends she invited over—

"It's Brad and his dad, Traci. She invited them—"

She sat up so fast her head started spinning. Her heart leaped into her throat, then began to pound with heavy precision. "She didn't!" Her voice sounded as if someone were strangling her.

"Calm down. I locked her in the basement."

Traci felt as if her eyes were going to pop out of her head. "You did *what?*"

"I locked her in the basement," Corky repeated matter-of-factly. "After she called them, she went down into the basement to get some jam—I think it was the strawberry your aunt made—"

"Get to the point, Corky!"

"Anyway, while she was down there, I locked the door."

Traci knuckled her eyes, praying that she was still dreaming. "You locked my mother in the basement."

"Isn't that what I said? Twice?"

"You can't do that!"

Corky looked offended. "Hey, I did it for *you.* They'll be here in fifteen minutes."

"Oh, God." Traci scrambled from the bed and frantically pawed through her closet for a pair of jeans and a T-shirt. "Go check on her while I get dressed," she ordered. "And don't let her see you."

"What are you going to do?"

"I don't know, but I'll think of something."

What *was* she going to do?

What a mess!

Chapter Twelve

She was tired of lying.

She wasn't very good at it anyway, and she really, really liked Brad. Which meant that eventually he would have to meet her mom, and he'd find out that Susan was the "ditzy redhead" who'd smashed into his dad's car.

Besides, after riding in the car with Ted Davidson, Traci pretty much believed they were both at fault. Susan had admitted she'd been distracted, and Traci had seen for herself how recklessly Ted Davidson drove.

And hadn't Brad agreed with her?

Deciding to grab the tiger by the tail, Traci marched downstairs to the basement door. Her mother was beating on the door and screaming to be let out. Traci took a deep breath, unlocked the door, and pulled it open.

Susan stood at the top of the stairs, holding a jar of homemade jam and looking exasperated. She also looked beautiful and younger than her years with her red hair tied in a ponytail. "My word! I can't believe I locked myself in the basement!" She rushed by Traci and into the kitchen. "They'll be here any minute, too. Pumpkin, will you get the good cloth napkins out?" Beaming at Traci, she added, "I've got a surprise for you. You might want to brush your teeth and comb your hair."

"Mom! I *did* comb my hair and brush my teeth!"

"Oh. Sorry, I keep forgetting that style's supposed to

look messy. In that case, will you heat the syrup and help me set the table?"

"Mom—"

"Hurry, pumpkin! Brad and his father are coming to breakfast!"

"Mom—"

"Brad's father sounded so nice on the phone. You didn't tell me that he was nice."

"Mom—"

"His voice sounded familiar, though. I've been racking my brain all morning trying to remember where I've heard that voice."

"Listen, Mom—"

"Maybe I met him when I was taking those karate classes? There were oodles of good-looking men there. Of course, most of them were married."

"Will you—"

"Honey, why aren't you helping me? You're just standing there like a bump on a log."

"I'm trying to tell you—"

"I know! I probably met him at that demonstration I helped organize. You know, the one at that market that was buying imported beef?"

Just as Traci opened her mouth to try again, the doorbell rang.

Susan squealed like a schoolgirl, grabbing Traci's hands and doing a little jiggle. "Oh! They're here! You answer the door while I start the waffles. I didn't want to make them too early, because who likes cold waffles?"

Traci swallowed her frustration and went to answer the door. Before she could take two steps, Susan grabbed her T-shirt and yanked her around.

Her mother's pretty brown eyes were gleaming with anticipation and unmistakable hope. "I can't stand the suspense. Tell me, pumpkin. Is Brad's father a hunk?"

So this was about meeting Brad's father, Traci mused. Not about meeting her daughter's new boyfriend. She should have known. "Yeah," Traci said honestly. "For an old guy, he's a hunk."

"Do I look okay?"

"You look beautiful, as always." So she sounded a little jealous. Maybe she was, because she felt compelled to add, "But don't get your hopes up. I don't think he's going to be your type."

Susan frowned. "Why would you say that?"

"You'll see."

Oh, boy, would she ever see. Traci dragged her feet answering the door, dreading the coming explosion. That there would be one, she had no doubt. She just wished she'd been honest with Brad so it wouldn't be such a shock. It wasn't fair to him.

The doorbell pealed again.

Too late now, Traci thought, chewing her bottom lip nervously. She unlocked the door and reluctantly pulled it open.

Brad looked relaxed and scrumptious, as usual. Ted, on the other hand, looked anxious.

"Hi," Brad said, flashing her one of his knee-weakening smiles. "Your mother invited us over for breakfast."

Traci's smile was genuine. How could it not be, when she was looking at Brad? "She told me."

Ted ran a distracted hand through his tousled blond hair. He wore it a bit longer than Brad's, but it looked good on him. "I have a weakness for waffles, so how could I resist?"

Convinced that he'd soon wished he *had* resisted, Traci moved aside and waved them in. She pointed to the kitchen doorway. "She's in the kitchen." When Ted started in that direction, Traci grabbed Brad's arm before he could follow. "I need to tell you something," she whispered.

Brad lifted a questioning eyebrow. "Sounds serious."

"It is." She glanced up just in time to see Ted disappear into the kitchen. She winced visibly. "My mom is the one who—"

"*You!*" came Ted's shocked bellow from the kitchen.

"*You!*" Susan echoed, just as loudly. "What are *you* doing in my house? How dare you . . . "

Traci groaned. She pushed Brad toward the door. "Come on. Let's wait outside until the war is over."

"War?" Brad looked totally lost. "What war?"

"The war between your dad and my mom." Traci opened the door and continued to push him outside.

When they'd both cleared the threshold, she firmly shut the door. She could still hear them shouting, but couldn't tell what they were saying. Honestly, she really didn't want to know.

"What's going on, Traci? Why is my dad and your mom fighting? They don't even know each other!"

"Um." Traci swallowed hard and stared at her bare feet. She didn't want to be looking at his face when she told him. "Yeah, they do. My mom is the woman who ran into your dad's BMW."

Brad sucked in a sharp breath, then let it out in a low, stunned whistle. "You're kidding."

"Not." Oh, how she wished she were!

"And you've known . . . how long?"

She rubbed one foot against the other, feeling miserable. "Since the day it happened. I just couldn't tell you."

"Why not?"

His voice was soft enough—nothing like his dad's at the moment—but Traci wasn't convinced that he didn't hate her for keeping it from him. She decided to come clean. What did she have to lose? "Because I was afraid you'd . . . that you'd . . . I don't know. Maybe not like me anymore?" Her voice ended on a silly squeaky note. She darted a quick look at him, then away again. She could tell nothing from his expression. Taking a deep breath, she added, "We'd just gotten together, remember? I didn't want to put a strain on our relationship." *Good grief!* She sounded like a soap opera!

She waited. He was silent so long she dared another glance at him. His shoulders were shaking. Traci frowned, her gaze traveling up his chest to his face.

He was laughing!

Her lips twitched. Could her luck be changing? "You're . . . you're not mad?"

Brad hooked a finger beneath her chin, still chuckling. "Why would I be mad? Your mom and my dad were involved in an accident. We've pretty much decided they were both at fault, haven't we?"

She nodded, so relieved she felt weak. He had that look in his eyes, the same look he had when he wanted to kiss her. Would he? Right here in broad daylight on her own front porch?

He bent his head closer, his eyelids drifting shut. Traci closed her eyes and parted her lips.

The front door opened abruptly. They sprang apart, staring at the empty doorway. Corky. It had to be Corky. She had forgotten about him! She started to go inside when something came flying out of the kitchen.

Splat! A gob of butter hit the hall wall opposite the kitchen doorway. It began to slide to the floor.

The voice of Susan shouted, "Get out of my house, you . . . you arrogant, overgrown teenager! Get out!"

Traci winced. Brad grinned. He was obviously

enjoying the show.

He cupped his hand around his mouth and whispered, "I think Dad's met his match, don't you?"

"She shouldn't call him—"

"I'd rather be an arrogant, overgrown teenager," Ted shouted as he backed out of the kitchen, "than a brainless—"

It was as far as Ted apparently dared to go. Hastily, he hurried down the hall and out the door without pause. He didn't stop until he was safely on the bottom step. His face was flushed red, but Traci noticed a peculiar gleam in his eyes when he turned to look through the door. *He's enjoying himself, too*, she thought, surprised and dumbfounded. Her father hated getting Susan riled.

"I was wrong," Ted muttered to no one in particular. "She really *is* a redhead. Would you get a load of that temper?"

As if on cue, another glob of butter hit the wall, followed by a frustrated scream.

"Brad, you can stay if you dare," Ted said. "I'm getting the heck out of here."

"Good idea, Dad. See you later." Brad waved cheerfully at his dad, still grinning from ear to ear. When the BMW pulled recklessly out of the driveway, Brad turned to Traci. "Should we go in and help clean up?"

"Yeah, I guess." Traci uttered a silent prayer that her mother wouldn't transfer her anger to Brad just because he was Ted's son. She didn't *think* her mother would, but these days Traci couldn't be sure of anything.

Just as they passed the stairs, loud music began to blare from her bedroom. Traci closed her eyes and ground her teeth.

Corky, of course. Who else?

"I'll just get that," she said, stifling a sigh. "I guess I left my alarm on. You can wait here if you'd rather." She figured anyone would rather wait than face her mother right now.

But she figured Brad wrong.

"I'll just go on in and introduce myself."

"Okay." Traci lifted both eyebrows. "Suit yourself, Brave Brad, but don't say I didn't warn you."

Brad pulled her to him and planted a quick kiss on her open mouth. He grinned down at her. "I'm not that brave. Just hungry."

"Oh." One little bitty kiss and she was speechless. And pathetic. "Be . . . be careful."

"I will."

She watched him for a moment, her heart fluttering and her mouth still tingling. Yep. She was definitely in love. Now if she just knew how to keep him interested. All in all, she thought she was pretty dull, despite all the recent activity going on around her. But those activities were just life's little ironic coincidences, right?

She trudged upstairs, her head bent, thinking about Brad and how happy she was when she was with him.

As she cleared the last step, the music stopped abruptly.

So did Traci. With a rueful shake of her head, she walked the last few steps to her bedroom.

"What took you so long?" Corky demanded, scaring a year off her life by popping out in front of her. "I thought you were going to help me, Trace."

"I am. Shh! Would you keep your voice down? Do you want them to hear you?"

Corky shrugged, but waited until she shut the door before he spoke again. "How long is *he* going to be here?"

Traci put her hands on her hips and narrowed her eyes. It was time she and Corky had a little talk about Brad.

Chapter Thirteen

"Please tell me what you have against Brad. I'd love to hear it." Okay, so maybe she should can the sarcasm for the time being. "Really," she added sincerely.

Corky cast her a baleful look before flopping onto her bed. The action momentarily scattered him. When he was back together again, he propped his head on his elbow and looked at her.

"He just, um, seems sneaky to me," he said.

"*Seems* sneaky?" Traci held on to her patience and crossed her arms, leaning her back against the door. Just a precaution in case someone decided to come barreling in and caught a ghost lounging on her bed. "Define sneaky."

"Not on the up-and-up. The makings of a two-timer, you know."

No, she didn't know, but just the thought made her heart ache. It wasn't easy to say, "We're not officially boyfriend/girfriend, Corky. We're both free to date other people."

Corky lifted a disbelieving eyebrow. "And you're okay with that?"

She tapped her toe against the carpet, refusing to answer on the grounds that it might incriminate her. When Corky remained silent, she blew out an exasperated breath. "All right, Corky. You win. Do you know something I don't? If you do, then spill it and stop beating around the bush."

"Not *really*," he said with frustrating vagueness. He

pulled a magazine from her nightstand and began to flip through the pages.

Traci got the impression he was avoiding looking her in the eye. A shiver of premonition swept down her spine. "Corky?"

He sighed and slapped the magazine closed. "No, I don't know anything that you don't know. I just don't trust him."

"You're jealous," Traci stated, softening her voice. Why wouldn't he be? Before he died, they had been exploring a deeper relationship. Granted, it hadn't gone far, but . . .

With a snort, Corky sat up. "Are you out of your mind? You think I don't know that I'm a ghost? Even if I *were* jealous, what good would it do me?" He made a face. "It's obvious you're crazy about the guy, Trace."

"But you know something and you're not telling me." Suddenly Traci was convinced she was right. Her tummy lurched. For a moment she thought she was going to be sick; then the nausea subsided. "Is . . . is he seeing someone else?"

Corky flashed her a startled glance, then focused on the front cover of her *YM* magazine. "Um, no, not that I know of. Why would he, when he's got the greatest girl in the world?"

Traci's heart melted. She sat on the edge of the bed, aching to touch him. But she didn't like that cold feeling; it reminded her that he was dead. Dead and gone to her.

She swallowed a burning knot in her throat. "I'm . . . I'm sorry things didn't work out for you," she said softly.

Corky ducked his head. "Yeah. Me, too." He looked up at her, his eyes burning and full of determination. "But I think I know why I came back."

"You do?"

"Yeah. I think I came back to save Mom."

Inwardly, Traci groaned.

"You'll help me, like you promised?" Corky asked hopefully, his earlier surliness gone. "You'll talk to that deserting bum?"

"Yeah. I promised, didn't I?" She jumped up from the bed. "Right now I'm going to go downstairs and save Brad from Mom."

Chuckling, Corky opened the magazine again. "Yeah, you'd better get down there. I don't think I've ever seen Susan so mad." He frowned in thought. "Except for that time we dyed all her underwear blue."

Traci giggled. "Yeah, she was pretty mad."

"Not as mad as *I* was when she made us *wear* it around the house."

They burst out laughing.

Traci was still smiling when she went downstairs.

"Want another waffle, honey? More syrup? Sorry about the butter . . . "

She ground to a halt on the bottom step, her jaw dropping. Her mother sounded . . . *normal*. Unfortunately, that wasn't always a good thing.

"Thanks, but I think I'll wait on Traci. The waffles are great, though."

At Brad's polite response, Traci relaxed slightly. She continued down the hall to the kitchen. Brad hadn't sounded awed or entranced at all. Apparently her mother's considerable charms didn't appeal to him.

As they had to Adam, and just about every other guy she knew who had met her beautiful mother. Could she get so lucky? The crappy part about guys going bananas over her mother was that she didn't really blame them. Compared to Susan, she was a plain Jane.

"Pumpkin!" Susan cried the moment she spotted her. "I'm sorry about that scene, and I've already apologized to Brad."

"Three times," Brad inserted, his gaze locked on Traci. "I told her that she didn't have to apologize. My dad can be a jerk sometimes."

Traci pulled out a chair opposite Brad and sat, unable to take her eyes from Brad. "Yeah, well, Mom can be a little *over*dramatic sometimes, too." Traci rolled her eyes, making Brad grin.

"Traci!" Susan slapped a waffle onto Traci's plate. "I'll have you know I have every right to be angry with Brad's father. He didn't even consider that he might have been at least *partially* responsible for the accident."

"Sounds like Ted," Brad said, further energizing her mother. He winked at Traci, but Traci just gave a furtive shake of her head that clearly said, *Please don't encourage her!*

"See? Even Brad thinks it was his father's fault." Susan sounded smug and very pleased that Brad had taken her side. She sat at the head of the table and began pouring syrup onto her steaming waffle. "And he understands why I'm forbidding you to get into the car with that maniac—sorry, Brad—again."

"Mom!" Traci dropped her fork, smearing syrup on her jeans as she fought to catch it before it hit the floor. She felt her face heating up. "You're talking about Brad's father, you know."

Susan shrugged. "So? He knows his dad's a bad driver."

It couldn't go on this way. It just couldn't. Knowing she was heading for hot water, Traci reminded her mother, "Have you forgotten what *you* were doing when you plowed into Mr. Davidson's BMW?"

Her mother's face flushed. She kept her gaze on her plate. Traci expected her to start humming an innocent tune any second.

"Mom? Have you forgotten that you were repairing a nail, and that you had dropped the nail file, which in turn caused you to stomp on the gas pedal?" Traci looked at Brad, determined to be fair. "Did she tell you, Brad? Did she tell you she was going forty in a twenty-five-mile-an-hour zone?"

Brad looked uncomfortable. "Um, no. She didn't."

Susan cast her a sulky look. "Sheesh, Traci. You're making it sound like it was *all* my fault. He pulled out in front of me. If he hadn't been there, I wouldn't have hit him."

"What if someone else had been in front of you?" Traci prompted, expecting her mother to blow any second, but feeling an odd urge to take up for Ted.

Her mother let out an exasperated sigh and leaped to her feet. "Traci, I really hate it when you reverse the roles. I'm not your daughter, I'm your *mother*."

So start acting like it, Traci wanted to say, but knew she couldn't. She looked at Susan, standing by the table wearing hip-hugging pink denim and a hot pink peasant top that revealed her tanned midriff. When would she grow up and start acting like other moms? Traci was beginning to think it was *never* going to happen.

Tossing her head, Susan took on an injured look Traci was certain was designed to elicit Brad's sympathy.

"I'm going to my room," she announced with a sniff. "You guys can clean up."

With her beautiful head held high, Susan stomped out of the kitchen. Traci winced as her mother's bedroom door slammed shut with unnecessary force. She looked at Brad to find him watching her with a glimmer of accusation in his moss-green eyes. *Oh, great,* she thought, fighting the urge to let out a scream of frustration as her mother had earlier. But she *wasn't* her mother, and neither did she want to be.

"I think you hurt her feelings," Brad said softly, trying and failing to sound neutral.

"She does this on purpose," Traci said, at that moment wishing she'd chosen to live with her dad. "She makes me look like the bad guy so that everyone will feel sorry for her." She took a deep breath, wondering if this would be the end of their brand-new relationship. "And it worked, didn't it?"

"Traci—"

"That's okay, Brad." Traci's voice trembled as she rose and began gathering their plates to take to the dishwasher. "You don't know her the way I do. She got it wrong, you know, when she called your dad an overgrown teenager. *She's* the overgrown teenager." She slammed the dishes into the rack, her anger growing. Her mother had caused this—this argument! "She borrows my makeup, my clothes, and my CDs."

As if on cue, 'NSYNC music began to blare from her mother's bedroom. Traci threw out her hands.

"See what I mean?"

"She must have been young when she had you."

That was it? That was all he had to say? Traci closed her eyes and counted to ten. It didn't work. She didn't feel calmer, or soothed. "She was seventeen, but what does that have to do with her not growing up?"

Brad laced his fingers together and propped them under his chin, staring at her so intently Traci flushed.

"So you'd feel better if she wore polyester pantsuits and listened to country?"

"Yes!" Traci bit her lip. She hadn't meant to yell at him. "I'm sorry."

"That's okay." He got up and gathered up the dirty silverware, bringing it to the dishwasher. He smiled at her, showing her that he wasn't mad. "At the risk of making you jealous, my dad hates my music and makes fun of most of my clothes." His grin widened. "He doesn't, however, wear anything polyester—in public, anyway. I told him that if he did, I'd move back in with Mom."

Traci couldn't resist matching his grin. Brad's teasing manner made her feel foolish and judgmental. Was she being too hard on her mom? This wasn't the first time Brad had said something that made her stop and think.

Reluctantly, she confessed, "I think I'm a little jealous of her. Isn't that awful?" Brad looked incredulous, making Traci feel warm all over.

"Why would you be jealous of Susan? I mean, she's pretty—for an older woman—but you're a knock-out, Trace."

Trace. It was the first time Brad had used her nickname, the same nickname Corky had always used for her—when he wasn't calling her Bobcat. How would he feel about Brad's calling her Trace? She cast a nervous glance around, but saw nothing suspicious.

Her heart lodged in her throat as Brad moved closer. He tipped her chin, inspecting her features with a thoroughness that made her start to tremble. She loved it when he did the chin-tipping thing because it made her feel special. She didn't even mind it when he stared at her as if he were searching for flaws.

His voice was soft and serious as he said, "You know, Corky's a lucky guy."

As his words sank in, Traci's knees nearly buckled. Her eyes widened in shock as she stammered out, "Why . . . why do you say that?"

Chapter Fourteen

Why did he have to bring up Corky when she was certain he was about to kiss her? Traci groaned inwardly, recalling the sad expression on Corky's face when she accused him of being jealous of Brad.

"Corky's a lucky guy," Brad said, lowering his mouth a fraction of an inch at a time, "because he's known you all your life. I've only known you a few months." He moved another inch closer.

Traci's lips parted despite her attempt to keep them shut. She couldn't let Brad kiss her knowing Corky might be watching. It was too cruel.

"He's also lucky that he has someone like you for a friend."

She swallowed very softly, riveted by his intense green gaze. Maybe Corky was still in her room and she could sneak one little bitty kiss. Or maybe run her fingers through his gorgeous blond hair to see if it was as soft as it looked.

"In fact, I'm wondering if I'm a fool not to be jealous of big brother."

Her mouth went dry. Just beyond Brad, the syrup bottle rose from the table and moved through the air. It hovered over Brad's head in an unmistakably threatening way.

"Um." She grabbed his shoulders and pushed him to the left. "My . . . my mom could come back in any moment."

The syrup bottle followed.

Desperately, Traci began to pull him in the direction of the kitchen door. "Maybe you're right. Maybe I should go apologize to her." She flashed him an overly bright smile and shoved him through the doorway into the hall. "I'll call you later, okay? Tell your dad that I'm sorry about . . . about everything."

To her intense relief, he kept walking toward the door. With Corky behind her—hopefully—she could relax. She could even smile and wave.

"Dumb jock," Corky sneered from somewhere near her ear.

She jumped and shot around, glaring at the air. How could he make her feel sorry for him one moment, and furious the next? "He's not a dumb jock, Corky. He's a great guy, and I . . . I like him a lot."

"That's pretty obvious the way you flutter your lashes and look at him as if he were God's gift to women." Corky's form began to slowly solidify. He was sitting in the chair her mother had vacated, fiddling with the handle on the syrup bottle. "He's not good for you."

Traci angled her chin. "Well, that remains to be seen, doesn't it?"

"'Well, that remains to be seen, doesn't it?'" Corky mimicked, sounding amazingly like Traci.

"When did you become so bitter and . . . and *nasty*?" She took a seat at the table and crossed her arms.

Corky stared at the syrup bottle, his expression

tense and thoughtful. "I don't know. Maybe eating a ton of mud at the bottom of Crawford Lake had something to do with it."

Instant remorse scattered the last of Traci's anger. "I guess that might do it. Do you . . . want to talk about it?"

He darted her a quick glance, which revealed nothing. "Not much to talk about. Anyway, it's rather a moot point now, ain't it?"

"We . . . the police never really knew how you, um, drowned. You were a good swimmer, Corky."

He stirred restlessly in the chair. "My memories of that day are kinda muddy."

His quick grin over his bad pun did nothing to ease the tightness in Traci's throat. She could never find anything remotely comical about Corky's death. Ever.

Corky seemed to sense that. He sighed. "I lost my tennis shoe. You know it isn't safe to swim in that lake barefoot with all the bottles and broken glass kids throw in there."

"It isn't *safe* to swim in the lake at all," Traci said quietly. "Which is why they have a 'No Swimming' sign posted. Was it Reggae's idea?"

"What difference does it make?" Corky shrugged. "I don't even remember who suggested it. I just know we were having the time of our lives seeing who could get to the other side first. Then I felt my shoe slipping off, and dove down to get it. I got tangled in some old fishing line, Bobcat. Can you believe it? I managed to get the hook out of my toe, but by that time I didn't have enough air to get back to the top. I sucked in a bunch of water." His voice dropped. "I remember thinking that I needed to call out for Reggae, let him know I was in trouble. But I couldn't with all that water in my lungs." He glanced at her, his eyes widening to cartoon proportions. "Don't cry, Bobcat. I can't stand it when you cry."

"I'm not . . . " Traci wiped at her face, surprised when her hand came away wet. She reached for a napkin and dried her cheeks, feeling foolish. Any moment now, Corky would start making fun of her. Call her a baby.

But surprisingly, he didn't.

"I heard Mom telling the deserter that you had to see a shrink after I died."

"A . . . a couple of times." Traci swallowed, wishing she'd never asked him how it had happened. Now she couldn't get the image of it from her mind. Reggae hadn't spoken to anyone for weeks, and by that time Traci hadn't *wanted* to know the details. "And it wasn't a shrink," she clarified, mustering a baleful look for Corky's benefit. "It was a grief counselor the school brought in."

Corky rolled his eyes, and the tension in the air eased. "A shrink is a shrink is a shrink. Whatever."

Traci giggled. Corky laughed. Soon they were both gripping their sides, unable to contain their mirth. Tears were spilling from her eyes again, but she knew they were tears of laughter. She reached for another napkin and dabbed her eyes, still chuckling.

"What is going on in here?"

At the sound of her mother's voice, Traci shrieked and leaped to her feet, sending her chair crashing to the floor behind her. She whirled around, staring at her mother's bewildered face. Oh, no, she thought, *she's seen Corky!* How was she going to explain? "I . . . I . . . We . . . You—"

"Traci . . . " Susan approached her, frowning now. "You've been acting pretty strange lately. Are you okay? Should I take you to the emergency room and ask them to do a CAT scan?"

"I—"

"Because this isn't the first time I've caught you talking to yourself, pumpkin."

Talking to her . . . *Oh.* Traci swung around to stare at the empty chair Corky had obviously vacated in the nick of time. A cold nudge to the back of her leg told her just where he'd gone.

He was under the table. Was he invisible? Visible? Flickering? Smoky? *Laughing* at her predicament?

Probably all of the above, Traci decided with an inward shake of her head. *Corky strikes again!*

He was *so* not funny!

"Wanna trade my peanut butter and jelly for your ham and Swiss on rye?" Christine offered hopefully.

They were eating lunch on the school grounds, surrounded by chattering classmates and buzzing bees. Traci was tempted because she loved peanut butter and jelly, but in the end her willpower prevailed. She shook her head. "I'm trying to lose a few pounds. Corky thinks I'm fat."

"He *what?*"

"He thinks I'm fat."

"He's nuts!" Christine looked murderous. "What does he know, anyway? He's thirteen. Still a punk, in my opinion."

Obviously her friend hadn't gotten over the bra incident, Traci mused, wisely holding back a grin. "That's the point, Christine. He's still immature enough to tell me the truth. He's always been honest with me, just as I have always been honest with him."

Christine huffed. "Are you saying you and I aren't honest with each other?" she challenged.

Traci gave an inward groan. "Come on, Christine! Girls lie to each other all the time just to make each other feel good."

"So you think I'm fat and you're just not telling me?"

What? Traci shook her head, exasperated. "That's not what I'm saying at all. You know you're not fat!

I'm the one *who* needs to lose a few pounds."

"You do not!"

"Do too."

"Do not!"

"Let's change the subject before we ruin our lunch." Traci was relieved when Christine agreed. "What do you think of my plan to get Mrs. Evans out of the house? Think it will work?"

Christine took a huge bite of her sandwich. She chewed and swallowed before she responded. "I don't know, Trace. Mrs. Evans and your mom aren't exactly friends."

"But they're not enemies, either," Traci pointed out. "If we convince Mrs. Evans that she's doing *me* a favor, I don't think she'll say no."

"Does your mom know about your plans?"

Great. She *would* have to zero in on the biggest problem. "Not yet. I was thinking of telling her when Mrs. Evans arrived."

Christine nearly choked on her sandwich. "Bad idea! You're actually thinking of waiting until Mrs. Evans knocks on your door, primed and ready for a free perm given by your mother, who, I might add, has only been going to beauty school for two weeks, before you let your mom know you invited her?"

"Yep."

"Does revenge have anything to do with this?" Christine waved frantically at a bee intent on getting a bite of her jelly. "Shoo! Shoo! Go get your own lunch, you stupid bee!"

"Bees aren't stupid," Traci informed her. "They're actually very intelligent."

"Whatever." Christine pitched the rest of her sandwich back into her bag and rolled it up before setting it aside. "Who else will be there for this . . . this beauty party?"

"A few of Mom's friends. You know, Rebecca, Cee Cee, and probably that weirdo Bambi. Maybe Aunt Gillian, although her and Bambi do *not* get along."

"I thought her name was Babs," Christine said.

"Babs, Bambi, whatever. I just know she's way stranger than my mom."

"Your mom's not strange," Christine protested, as Traci knew she would. "She's cool."

"Whatever." Traci hoped Christine would let it drop. She didn't feel up to fighting about whether her mother was strange or not. She was strange and that was that. If Christine or any of her other friends who thought Susan was cool had to live with her mom they'd change their minds. Traci was convinced of this.

"Sounds like you've got it all worked out. But you're forgetting something very important."

Traci frowned. "I am?"

"You are."

Impatiently, Traci leaned forward. She hated it

when Christine made her guess, and Christine knew it. "Just tell me, okay? The bell's going to ring any moment."

"Brad!" Christine crowed. "Your date with Brad Saturday night. What are you going to tell him?"

Closing her eyes, Traci called herself every name synonymous with *stupid*. How could she have forgotten? Brad had asked her out before she'd thought up her brilliant plan to help Corky talk to his father. At the time she hadn't known about her mother's plan to practice beauty techniques on her unsuspecting friends.

"Didn't you say you got the feeling he had something special planned?" Christine reminded her, sounding far too happy about Traci's situation.

"Yeah," Traci said reluctantly. "So it's going to be a tough one to get out of."

"Well, you'll just have to make something up."

"No." Traci wasn't aware of her decision until she said the word *no*. She was tired of lying to everyone, especially Brad. If they were going to have a relationship, then she was determined it would be based on honesty and trust, like the one she'd had with Corky.

Squaring her shoulders, she opened her eyes and stared at Christine with dead certainty. "I'm going to tell Brad the truth."

"The truth?" Christine squeaked, wide-eyed.

"The truth," Traci confirmed, but her voice qua-
vered. "I'm going to tell him about Corky being a
ghost."

Chapter Fifteen

"Just remember, this was *your* idea," Brad said jokingly as he parked the Jeep and cut the engine. "I don't want your friend Corky paying my Jeep another visit."

Traci shot him a startled glance. "You . . . you knew that Corky let the air out of your tires?"

"Well, I wasn't exactly certain until now."

When she let out a betraying groan, Brad laughed.

"Hey, it's okay. I just hope you set him straight about tonight *before* he gets the wrong idea. I don't need any more unfortunate accidents."

"I will." Her face was flaming, and she couldn't look at him. He had suspected Corky all along, but had said nothing. What a guy! In fact, she was beginning to think he was far too good for her. All she'd done from almost the moment they'd met was lie to him.

"So why do they call it Widow's Point?" Brad asked, trailing his arm along the back of her seat.

He wasn't touching her, but Traci was very aware of how close his arm was to her neck. She fancied she could feel his body heat. "Um." She licked her dry lips, staring through the windshield at the moonlit view of the forest surrounding Widow's Point. In the dark, the tops of the trees reminded her of mountains. "On the other side of that guardrail there's a hundred-foot drop. The story is that one night four guys came up here after a bachelor party. They were standing in front of the van, drinking and toasting each other, when the van slipped out of gear and rolled forward, pushing them off the cliff."

Brad whistled. "Wow. I take it they were all married?"

She nodded. "Except for the one *about* to get married. I . . . I don't know if the story is true," she confessed. "But that's the current rumor of why it's called Widow's Point. Sad, huh?"

"Yeah. That's pretty awful." He drummed his fingers on the top of the seat. "Are you okay? You seem nervous about something."

What could she be nervous about? Her best friend was back from the dead and she was at Widow's Point for the first time in her life—with Brad Davidson, hunk extraordinaire. And she had to find a way to tell him Corky was a ghost. *Nope. Nothing to be nervous about!*

"I, um, have something to tell you."

"You can tell me anything, Trace," Brad said softly. "Whatever either of us has done in the past is history as far as I'm concerned. In fact—" He broke off, taking his class ring from his finger. He picked up her hand and slipped it onto her finger.

It was too big, but who cared?

"I was going to wait until Saturday night, but figured I might as well take advantage of the setting." His smile was lopsided and sweet. "I think I'm in love with you, Traci. I can't think of anything or anyone else but you."

She loved Brad too, but everything seemed so complicated! Traci stared at the beautiful class ring that hung loosely on her finger.

She was now officially dating Brad Davidson. It didn't matter to Brad that Adam had spread ugly rumors about her. It didn't matter to Brad that his dad and her mom were locked in a legal battle over a ridiculous accident. And it didn't matter that she had a mischievous boy *friend* who let the air out of his tires.

A *ghost* of a boy friend.

He thought he loved her, despite the huge obstacles in the way.

"This is it," she muttered, closing her hand so that the ring wouldn't slip off. "I have to tell him."

"Tell me what?" Brad prompted gently. "Come on, Traci. I care about you. You can tell me anything."

He had no idea what he was saying, Traci thought, feeling panic rise. She forcefully unglued her tongue from the roof of her mouth. "I told you about Corky."

"Yeah, and I told *you* that I envy him."

He sounded puzzled, even a little worried, she thought. Well, he should be. "I didn't tell you everything." Why couldn't she just say it? Tell him that Corky was a ghost?

"Oh."

She heard the disappointed sigh in his voice, and knew that he'd misunderstood her hesitation. She rushed to correct the problem. "No, no, he's not . . .

we're not . . . " She clenched her fist, feeling the ring biting into her palm. "Corky's a ghost," she finally blurted out. She kept her gaze steadfastly on the windshield in front of her. What was he thinking? Had she shocked him? Was he horrified? Did he think she'd gone nuts?

"A ghost," he repeated in a perfectly calm voice. "That would explain the way my shoelaces kept coming undone during the game, although I *know* that I tied them in a knot. That would also explain my helmet, and the fact that I felt as if someone was trying to pull down my pants."

Traci jerked her head in his direction, stunned. "You believe me? Just like that?"

Brad hesitated. "Well, I might not have, but all those weird things that happened . . . " His smile was rueful. "I thought I was going nuts. I'm relieved that there's a logical explanation."

"Logical?" Traci squeaked out, perversely wondering if Brad were the one losing his mind. It had taken her a lot longer to come to terms with the spooky fact that Corky was back. "How can you use the word *logical*? He's a *ghost*! I freaked out when I saw him, and so did Christine."

"I've had a little time to get used to the idea," Brad said. He picked up her hand and laced his fingers through hers. "That night that Dad picked us up and the car kept starting by itself reminded me of a story

Mom told me a few years ago. Her mom—my grandma—died when she was a teenager. A few months after she died, Mom went into the hospital to get her tonsils out. She said that when she woke up, she saw Grandma standing at the end of the bed. Grandma told her that she was just making sure she was alright. Then the light came on for the nurse, and Mom said she didn't push the button, that her hand wasn't anywhere near it."

"Oh." Traci was nearly speechless was shock. She didn't know what she'd been expecting, but it certainly wasn't this calm acceptance and a ghost story of his own.

"So tell me about him. Why is he here?"

"Funny you should bring that up," Traci said hoarsely. "Because that's what I wanted to talk to you about."

"Wait. There's something I've been wanting to do from the moment I picked you up tonight."

Before she could question his mysterious statement, he leaned forward and captured her lips in a wonderful, lingering kiss. By the time he broke free, her eyes were closed and her breathing was shallow. Her heart was beating a joyful melody that she thought he could surely hear.

"Wow," she breathed out loud. She wasn't aware that he'd heard her until he chuckled.

"Yeah, wow. I feel like that every time I kiss you."

She stared into his shadowed expression. "Me, too."

He grinned, leaning forward to tuck a strand of hair behind her ear, his hand lingering on her cheek. "You're like no other girl I've ever met, Traci."

She wanted him to kiss her again. She wanted him to kiss her for the next two hours. Opening her mouth with every intention of sharing her fantasy with him, she was suddenly blinded by headlights.

Simultaneously they both looked behind them, squinting at the car that had pulled in close behind the Jeep. Traci's first thought was, *Not Corky again!* But then she remembered that Corky was only thirteen and didn't know how to drive. Just another couple looking for some privacy, she assured herself, exchanging a puzzled glance with Brad.

Then the car door opened and a uniformed cop stepped out, his stocky form outlined by the headlights.

He was heading their way.

"I don't believe this," she muttered, feeling her face heat up. "What would a cop be doing out here? We're not even in the city limits!"

"Just be cool," Brad said, rolling down his window.

Traci tried to take comfort in the fact that Brad didn't sound worried at all.

The humiliation was eating her alive.

She stood in the living room while Officer Madden

and Susan discussed her and Brad as if they weren't there. What was wrong with her mother? What had happened to the coolest mom in town? Because the frowning woman who was shooting her killing glances wasn't *anything* like the mom she knew and hated.

Well, she didn't hate her mother, just despised the way she acted sometimes. Okay, most of the time.

She wasn't too happy with the way she was acting now, either.

"What were they doing when you pulled up behind them?" Susan was asking.

Her mother had one hand anchored firmly on her cocked hip, a sure sign that she was agitated. Traci felt her face heat another ten degrees. She couldn't keep quiet any longer. "I can answer that, Mom—"

"Silence!" Susan sliced her hand in the air, glaring at her. "I asked Officer Madden, not you." She folded her arms across her chest irately and fairly seethed as she waited for the uncomfortable officer to answer.

Traci nearly bit her tongue in two.

"Um, it appeared that they were . . . kissing, ma'am."

Officer Madden's face turned red. Traci took small comfort in the fact. "Mom, would you just listen to me? I can explain everything!" When Susan swung her way and began tapping a toe impatiently on the floor, Traci suddenly lost the ability to speak.

Her mother looked positively furious.

"Okay, missy. Explain to me why you were up at Widow's Point with Brad—and don't think I don't know what kids do up there—when you were supposed to be at the movies with Christine."

Oh, great. What was she supposed to tell her mother now that she finally had her attention? *If only Christine were here,* Traci thought, for once yearning for her friend's nervous chatter. Christine would have thought of a perfectly reasonable excuse for being at Widow's Point with Brad.

But Christine wasn't here.

Traci took a deep breath. Better that her mom think she was a lunatic than to think she'd been making out with Brad. "The truth is I was telling Brad about Corky, and—"

"And how close the two of them were when he was alive," Brad quickly inserted.

She felt the slightest pressure of his arm against hers, and a warm, wonderful feeling flooded her body. Brad had come to her rescue!

"You see, it was my idea to go up to Widow's Point so that we could talk privately," Brad continued.

Traci tried not to look amazed at his slightly guilty, bad-boy expression.

"But I had the best of intentions, Mrs. Nettleton. She wanted to tell me about Corky, and I wanted to ask her to wear my class ring." He gently took Traci's hand and held it up for Susan to see. "Yes, we were kissing, but I would never make Traci do anything she didn't want to do."

Just as Traci was about to let out a sigh of relief, she caught her mother's expression. She almost swallowed her tongue dragging the air back into her lungs.

It was obvious her mother didn't believe him! What was going *on?* Why was her mother acting as if she knew something *they* didn't even know? Unless . . . unless someone had aroused her suspicions . . .

Someone like *Corky.*

"Traci's father didn't force me to do anything I didn't want to do," Susan said, still eyeing Brad as if she wanted to scratch out his eyes. "Because he was very talented in *sweet-talking* me into it." When Traci's jaw dropped, Susan flushed. "I just don't want you doing something you'll regret, Traci."

"Mom! I told you we were only kissing! Why don't you believe me? What happened to your promise to trust me until I gave you a reason not to?"

Susan stared hard at her for a long moment, then sighed. Her earlier tension seemed to flow out of her. "I'm sorry, pumpkin. You're right. You haven't given me a reason not to trust you." The look she shot Brad, however, didn't exactly shout *trust.* "But after that call I got—"

"What?" Traci and Brad asked simultaneously.

Frowning, Susan looked from one alarmed face to the other. "I got a call from some boy tonight. He said that he was a friend of yours, Traci, and was concerned about some rumors he'd heard at school."

"Rumors?" Traci parroted, inwardly seething. Corky was *so* going to get it for this latest stunt! That Corky was behind the call Traci now had no doubt.

A quick glance at Brad told her he was thinking the same thing.

"He said that Brad had a reputation for seeing how fast he could get a girl up to Widow's Point," Susan finished, sounding more uncertain by the second.

Traci was positive their astounded expressions went a long way toward causing Susan's uncertainty. She blew out an exasperated breath, her gaze shooting to Officer Madden, who was listening with avid interest. His presence reminded her that she lived in a small town, one that thrived on gossip. "Mom, Brad's never been to Widow's Point before tonight."

Brad reinforced her statement by looking earnest and crossing his heart. "I swear, Mrs. Nettleton."

Officer Madden snorted.

Susan, Traci, and Brad all turned to glare at him. Her mother stomped to the door and opened it. "Thank you, Officer, for finding my daughter for me. I'll take it from here."

"Sure you don't want me to escort the young man home?" He stared pointedly at Brad as he spoke.

"Don't be ridiculous," Susan snapped, as if she hadn't been on the verge of throwing Brad out of the house herself just moments earlier. "Didn't you hear my daughter? She said that nothing happened, and my daughter doesn't lie to me."

The sound of the door shutting on Officer Madden luckily drowned out the sound of Traci's guilty moan.

"Do you, Traci?" Susan asked softly.

Or maybe not. Traci swallowed hard and stared at her mother, trying to look innocent. "Wh-what?"

"Do you lie to me? *Have* you lied to me?"

Traci managed to shake her head, feeling the heat leap into her face. It hadn't been gone long.

Slowly Susan crossed her arms and leaned against the door. She looked at Brad, then back to Traci. The mixture of concern and lingering suspicion in her eyes made Traci want to squirm.

"Is there something you'd like to tell me, pumpkin? Is that sick boy still bothering you? The one who tried to convince you he was Corky? Because if he is, you can tell me. There are laws against harassment, and they apply to teenagers as well."

Yeah, Traci thought, wondering how she was going to get out of this latest mess, but did those laws apply to *ghosts?*

Chapter Sixteen

Traci glanced at the kitchen clock for the tenth time. Where was Mrs. Evans? She was ten minutes late. Her mother had already started on Babs's highlights. Traci suppressed a smile over Babs's tortured expression as Susan yanked strands of hair through the tiny holes in the cap as if she were digging potatoes.

Cee Cee, who was leaning against the counter sipping on a cup of green tea, had opted to get her frizzy dark hair straightened, while Rebecca reluctantly volunteered to let Susan try her hand at French braiding.

In Traci's opinion, Rebecca had taken the safest route, and even *that* was iffy.

Sitting beside her at the kitchen table, Christine nudged her with her foot, then stared pointedly at the clock.

They both jumped as the doorbell rang.

"I'll get it!" Traci shouted, jumping to her feet. Christine was hot on her heels as Traci headed down the hall to answer the door.

"Maybe Gillian changed her mind," Susan said, her voice drifting after Traci. "I was looking forward to giving her that perm."

"Did you hear that?" Christine whispered, grabbing Traci's shirttail and giving it a sharp tug. "Maybe Susan won't be as mad as you think about Mrs. Evans showing up."

Traci hoped she was right. And if she wasn't, well,

then that was fine. She owed her mom one for inviting Brad and his dad over for breakfast without warning her. Pasting a bright smile on her face, Traci opened the front door.

Mrs. Evans looked nervous, but she mustered a smile as Traci took her hand and pulled her inside. "I hope I'm not too late?"

"No, um, not at all. Mom's waiting for you in the kitchen." With Christine giggling uncontrollably, Traci led the unsuspecting Mrs. Evans into the kitchen to join Susan, Cee Cee, Rebecca, and Babs, who wore a shark's tooth earring, of all things, through her eyebrow.

The moment she appeared in the doorway with Mrs. Evans, all conversation halted abruptly. Susan's jaw dropped. She stared at Corky's mom as if she were a . . . well, a ghost. Traci attempted to hide her nervousness with another way-too-fake smile. "Mom, look who's here. Mrs. Evans, Corky's mom."

Susan closed her jaw, but recovered slowly. "Yes, I see that, Traci." The sharp, pointed glance she shot Traci promised retribution at a later date. "Blanche . . . how are you?"

"Just dandy. How have you been?"

"Great. Wonderful. What can I do for—"

"Mom, don't you remember? Mrs. Evans is here for her perm." Traci sucked in her bottom lip as Susan's jaw dropped *again*. In a rush, she added,

"She wants it to look loose and natural, and I told her you were just the person to do it. She wants to surprise *Mr.* Evans with a new hairdo, so I'll leave you to it. Christine and I are, um, going for a walk. You girls have fun!"

This time Traci got the opportunity to do some yanking on Christine. She yanked her speechless friend down the hall and through the kitchen door before her mother had the chance to say boo.

The moment the door was shut, Traci let out a shaky breath and wiped her brow. "Whew! That was scary! Did you see the way Mrs. Evans was staring at Babs's shark tooth?" Before Christine could answer, she grabbed her arm and hauled her off the porch. They started at a brisk clip in the direction of Corky's house. "You'd think she'd never seen a pierced eyebrow before. Or maybe she's never seen one on a woman Babs's age."

They were halfway there before Christine found her voice. "You are in so much trouble, my friend."

"I know." Traci shrugged, continuing to drag her friend along. They didn't have time to waste. The way Traci figured it, anything could happen in that kitchen over the next five minutes. She would worry about her own hide later. "Come on, Christine. You've got the list, right?"

"Of course I've got the list. You gave it to me, didn't you?"

"You don't have to get smart about it."

"And *you* don't have to yank my arm out of its socket!" Christine dug her heels into the pavement and leaned backward until Traci let go. She rubbed her arm. "That's better. I don't know why you're doing this for that punk anyway, after what he did to you and Brad."

Traci stopped herself before she ground her teeth. She couldn't think about the Widow's Point incident without wanting to scream. "I don't want to talk about it. Besides, I may be mad at Corky, but I promised him I would help."

"Yeah, but *I* didn't," Christine pointed out as they arrived at Corky's front door.

Traci jabbed the doorbell before she chickened out. To think she had given up a date with Brad for *this*. Not only would she be grounded for the rest of her life, she was about to interrogate a man who drilled holes in the ocean floor for a living.

Christine continued to get on her already frayed nerves with her whining.

"What if he doesn't believe us? What if he laughs in our faces and throws us out?"

"He won't. He's always been nice to me, and besides, Corky gave him a wedgie."

"And your point *is?*"

Footsteps could be heard approaching the door. Traci tried to calm her jittery nerves. "If reminding him of that doesn't work, then I've got a backup plan."

"And you forgot to share it with *me*?"

The door opened, putting an end to Christine's chatter. Mr. Not-so-wonderful stood on the threshold looking politely quizzical.

"What can I do for you girls?"

Get another life, Traci thought, but didn't say. She wiped her sweaty palms on her jeans and launched into her speech. "We'd like to come in and talk to you about something important, Mr. Evans."

"Oh?" He frowned, but didn't invite them in. "What's this about?"

"Corky," Traci said bluntly. She didn't have time to be gentle. "Can we please come in?"

"How do you know *he's* not listening?" Christine asked in a loud whisper the moment Mr. Evans disappeared to get them Cokes. They were huddled together on the love seat in the den.

"Because he promised me that he'd stay in his room." Traci kept her burning gaze on the empty doorway. "Give me the list." When Christine placed the crumpled list in her hand, Traci glanced down at it. She carefully smoothed it out with her fingers and took a deep, fortifying breath.

"I'm afraid all we have is diet," Mr. Evans said as he came back into the room.

Traci jerked, tearing a corner of the paper. "That's . . . that's fine," she stammered. Now that the moment had come, she honestly didn't know if she could go through with it. Suddenly her plan seemed silly and outrageous.

But she couldn't back out now. She couldn't let Corky down, no matter how many awful stunts he had pulled. Besides, she knew that Corky was just being protective of her, a trait she had once found endearing. He didn't want Brad to hurt her.

Christine nudged her with her elbow, then cleared her throat loud enough to sound embarrassingly obvious.

"Traci?" Mr. Evans prompted.

"Wh-what?" Traci felt her eyes getting bigger and bigger. She stared at the man's apprehensive expression, willing her mouth to move again. "I . . . I—"

"Oh, for heaven's sake," Christine snapped, grabbing the list from her hand and taking the bull by the horns in her usual, startling way. "Mr. Evans, we're here to tell you that your son has come back as a ghost. He's upstairs in his room right now, waiting on us to finish this interview. He would be here in per—um—be here, but we don't want you having a heart attack on us like *I* nearly did when I saw him for the first time."

Traci sat there, amazed, as Christine let out a hearty laugh in remembrance. Mr. Evans was beginning to look alarmingly pale.

"I nearly peed my pants when I—" A not-so-subtle jab to the ribs from Traci got her back on track. "Oh, yeah. Anyway, why we're here. You see, it was just Corky and his mom for a long time, and Corky's afraid you're going to break his mother's heart again."

"I'll . . . I'll take it from here, Christine." Traci said hoarsely. She took the list from Christine again. "He wants us to ask you some questions."

Mr. Evans gave his head a disbelieving shake. "I'm glad my wife isn't here. This would upset her." He stood, looking sternly down at them. "You two should be ashamed, pulling a stunt like this."

"He gave you a wedgie," Traci blurted out. "When you were in his room, crying."

The man's stern expression faltered for a brief second, then hardened again. "I don't know what you're talking about. Please leave."

But Traci had come too far to back out over a little disbelief. She implemented the backup plan, praying that Mr. Evans didn't have a heart condition.

Or a spasmodic bladder.

"Corky said that if you didn't believe us, I was to tell you that he knows about your, um, your . . . " Okay, so maybe it wasn't going to be exactly easy. She took a deep breath and braced herself. "He knows about your . . . hemorrhoid problems."

182

His face went from pale to dark red in about two seconds flat. His expression turned thunderous. "Have you actually been *spying* on us?" he demanded.

Christine uttered a tiny squeak and pressed into Traci, whispering, "I think we should get out while the gettin' is good!"

"No." Traci thrust out her chin, determined not to cower. Corky would be disappointed in her if she did, she knew. "*We* haven't been spying on you, but Corky has. He knows a lot of things about you that we couldn't know. Like the fact that you talk in your sleep, and you keep a picture of Corky in your wallet, the one where he's holding a baby rabbit you got him for Easter when he was three."

Mr. Evans, looking pale again, sat down abruptly in the chair behind him. He wiped his hand over his face, staring at them with the shocked eyes of someone who has heard terrible — or unbelievable — news.

Traci felt a surge of triumph. "Do you believe us now, Mr. Evans?"

He shook his head again. "I don't . . . know. How else could you know about the picture? And that I talk in my sleep? Even Blanche doesn't know I have that picture in my wallet. And . . . and I did feel something in his room that day."

"That was Corky giving you what you deserve," Christine piped up, earning a quelling glare from Traci. She looked sulky. "Well, he does."

"She's right. I did deserve it."

Both girls stiffened in surprise at his confession.

Mr. Evans got up and began pacing, shoving his hands in his pockets. "I shouldn't have run out on them like that, and that's something I've got to live with."

Maybe, Traci thought hopefully, she wouldn't even have to ask the questions. Maybe the man was going to answer them all on his own.

She kept quiet, and warned Christine to do the same by nudging her sharply with her elbow.

"I suppose he wants to know why?" Mr. Evans paused long enough to look at them.

Traci hastily nodded.

"He has a right to know, and I owe it to him. I just wished I could have told him before . . . " His voice cracked, and for one awful moment his face crumpled. But he rallied and swallowed hard, continuing to pace in front of them. "This is going to sound bizarre."

After the week she'd had, Traci highly doubted it.

Mr. Evans sat abruptly, dangling his hands between his knees and leaning forward. "I was never on an oil rig, like Blanche and Corky believed," he said bluntly. "I've been doing undercover work for the government that involved a lot of time and money, and it was decided that to keep my family safe, it was best that I have no contact with them. The assignment took longer than we expected."

Christine's eyes nearly swallowed her face. "Wow. You mean you're a spy?"

Traci, on the other hand, wasn't buying it. There were too many holes in his story, as far as she was concerned, and she was positive Corky would feel the same way. "Come on, Mr. Evans. No assignment lasts *that* long."

He made a show of concession. "You're right; it doesn't, but when it was over, my superiors warned me it would be dangerous to come home right away. You see, if my enemies recognized me, I'd be leading them straight to my family." He lifted his hands in a helpless gesture and let them fall. "To Blanche and Corky, and they didn't deserve that."

"Well, that should satisfy the punk—"

Traci clamped her hand over Christine's smart mouth. "And Mrs. Evans just took you back with open arms?"

"She hasn't asked me a thing."

"Which is why Corky didn't know," Traci murmured, mostly to herself. She frowned. "He thinks you're after his mom's savings, and he's not too cool on the fact that you're trying to get her to sell the house and move away."

"I've got my own money, and there's still a chance that my cover could be blown and my enemies—friends and family of the scum I've helped put away—could trace me back to Beachmont. If that happens, then we wouldn't be safe here."

"So you're no longer working undercover?" Traci asked, still skeptical, but beginning to consider that he might be telling the truth. Yes, it was bizarre, but so was Corky coming back as a ghost, and *somebody* had to work for the government. Why not Mr. Evans?

"I quit. I told them I'd given up too much already, and that I was going to go home and make it up to my family." Tears flooded his eyes. He wiped a hand over his face, and Traci saw that it was trembling. "Unfortunately, I was too late to make it up to Corky, but I'm going to do everything I can to make it up to Blanche."

"Wow," Christine said again. It seemed to be the only thing she was capable of saying.

"Do you have any proof?" Traci asked, suspecting Corky would be harder to convince. His hurt went deep, and his suspicion had had enough time to put down roots that would be hard to shake loose.

Mr. Evans hesitated, then got up. "I have something to show you. I'll be right back."

"Wow," Christine breathed for the third time as Mr. Evans left the room. "I wish my dad were a spy."

"Government agent, Christine. He was a government agent, not a spy. And I'm sure Corky would rather have had a garbage man for a dad than to not have one at all." Traci hated to be a drag, but she knew that was how *she* would feel. "So before you start worshiping the ground he walks on, you might consider Corky's feelings."

"Why should I? Did that punk consider *your* feelings when he called your mom and convinced her Brad was taking you to Widow's Point to jump your bones? Did he consider *my* feelings when he unhooked my bra in front of a hundred people at that football game?"

"Shh! He's coming back."

Traci tensed as Mr. Evans entered the room. He was carrying a small briefcase. He handed it to her with a sad, fleeting smile.

"There's your proof. Take it to his room and show it to him; then I'll have to burn it. I should have done it sooner, but something told me to wait."

Christine's eyes were bright as she snatched the briefcase from Traci's hands and jumped up. "Come on. I'm dying to see what's inside. It's probably full of neat spy stuff."

Without waiting to see if Traci followed, she headed to Corky's room.

With a long-suffering sigh, Traci trailed after her friend. But she was also wondering: What *was* in that briefcase?

Chapter Seventeen

They all stared at the items in the briefcase lying in the middle of Corky's bed for a long, silent moment.

Corky spoke first. "Anybody with half a brain could make a couple of fake IDs and a badge."

But Traci heard the reluctant admiration he tried to conceal. It was time to help Corky believe, she decided. Right or wrong, she felt that Mr. Evans was telling the truth. "Give him a break, Corky. He was just doing his job."

"And ignoring his wife and child." Corky gave her a strangely pitying look. "You're too trusting, Bobcat."

Now, where had *that* come from? *She* was too trusting? Traci narrowed her eyes. "What do you mean by that remark?"

"Yeah," Christine added. "Just what did you mean by that?"

Corky's gaze slid from Traci's, further arousing her suspicions. A nasty shiver rolled down her spine. "Corky?" she prompted softly. Once again she got the feeling that he was hiding something from her, something she probably didn't really want to know.

"Never mind," Corky mumbled. He fingered the stack of plastic cards portraying his father in different disguises with different names.

Traci reached out and smacked his hand, causing a smattering of crackling sparks to fly in all directions as his fingers disintegrated, then slowly formed again. "Tell me, Corky. You're hiding something and friends don't do that to each other." She softened her voice. "True friends don't, anyway."

"You'll hate me for telling you."

"I'll hate you if you *don't* tell me," she countered. Her stomach was flip-flopping around, making her queasy. "It's about Brad, isn't it?" For once Christine remained silent. Waiting, as she was waiting.

"You'll freak," Corky stated.

So it *was* about Brad. "No, I won't," she lied. She probably would, but not in front of Corky.

He turned his back on her and sat on the bed, as if he couldn't stand to watch her reaction to his news. She knew by the way his shoulders were slumped that he took no joy in the telling.

"I had to get out of the house while you talked to my dad, so I walked into town."

When Corky let the silence stretch, Traci filled in the blanks. "You saw Brad."

Christine let out a tiny squeak, then fell silent again.

"Yeah, I saw the creep. He was with some blond chick at Charlie's Pizza. They—they were sitting real close."

Traci heard a cracking sound, and knew it was her heart breaking. She had broken a date with Brad to help Corky, and he'd found someone else.

What a guy.

What a disloyal creep of a guy.

How could she have been so wrong about him?

She felt the outline of the ring she'd stuck in her jeans pocket for fear of losing it. It didn't make sense! Why would he give her his class ring, then find another girl the moment her back was turned? And he'd taken that girl to a public place, knowing everyone would see them together.

Knowing someone would tell her, and there were a few who would take great glee in telling her. Like Adam.

At least the news had come from someone who cared about her, who truly hated to see her hurt. She felt cold hands come to rest on her shoulders.

"Don't worry, Bobcat," Corky whispered. "I'm going to dedicate the rest of my foggy days to haunting Brad Davidson. I'll make him wish he'd never hurt my best friend."

Christine gave a sympathetic sniff. "I might end up liking you after all, Corky, and that's *my* best friend, thank you very much."

"*Our* best friend," Corky corrected, and surprisingly, Christine didn't argue.

Tears threatened, making Traci's eyes burn. She needed to go home, to her room where she could cry without an audience.

Brad had found someone else.

And he didn't even have the guts to tell her.

* * * *

The bloody knife sticking from Traci's chest looked real enough. She had the pain to go along with it, so she wasn't surprised when people took a second look at her crazy costume as she pushed through what appeared to be everyone in her sophomore class, and quite a few people she only vaguely recognized.

Susan had long ago earned the reputation for giving the best Halloween party in town. If you wanted to have a great time, eat gross-looking food, listen to great music, and see the scariest costumes, 1112 Elderberry Street was the place to come. There was a little matter of giving a small donation at the door for Susan's current cause, but most people didn't mind.

Traci grabbed a cup of punch from the party table, fished out a bloodshot candied eyeball, and dropped it into the nearest wastebasket. It didn't matter to her if the candy tasted like wild cherries—she wasn't eating anything that could stare back at her.

She caught sight of Christine, who made a pretty decent vampire, standing by the door with a menacing expression on her bloodless face.

She bared her fangs as Traci reached her, hissing, "I just vant to suck your blood."

"In your dreams," Traci said, taking a sip of her punch and wishing she could sneak up to her room and continue her three-day crying jag. Alone. "Mom got you on door patrol or something?"

Christine snatched her punch and took a thirsty

swallow before answering. "Adam Luke's here. Susan thought she saw him getting money *out* of the bucket, instead of dropping something in."

"Really?" Traci could care less. Her heart felt numb, yet on fire at the same time. It was a confusing contradiction. "What's the charity this year?"

"She didn't tell you?"

"Probably. I wasn't listening." But she had heard the phone ring—all twenty-seven times. Brad had finally given up around ten o'clock the night before.

The sudden silence had been worse than listening to the incessant ringing.

"She's trying to raise enough money to send the entire fourth grade to Six Flags amusement park in St. Louis."

Traci snorted. "Figures. She doesn't even have a child in the fourth grade."

"Rebecca does."

"That explains it." Traci reclaimed her punch as the voice of Sheryl Crow blared from the stereo speakers. A couple of ghouls arrived, stopping to drop money in the umbrella bin placed strategically by the door. At this rate, Traci thought, catching sight of the fifty-dollar bill lying on top of the pile, the entire grade school would be going to Six Flags.

"So . . . how many times did Brad call today?" Christine asked as she studied her long black nails.

Traci's stomach clenched. She took a deep breath,

forcing herself to relax. It was over. She needed to face it and get on with her life. "None. I think he wore the phone out."

"Lucky you."

How was *that* lucky? He was most likely dying to fill her head with a bunch of lies about why he was with a beautiful blonde at Charlie's.

"Look." Christine nudged her, then pulled her aside to let another guest through. "It's someone dressed as the Undertaker. I'll bet Corky would turn over in his . . . um . . . would flip if he saw that." She let out a startled screech as the Undertaker spread his arms and reached for her.

"*Nobody* wears this costume but *me*," Corky said in a mock-menacing growl. He threw his other arm around Traci. "Think anyone will recognize me?"

"Let's hope not," Traci said dryly. "And you know it won't be fair if you get best costume."

"What?" Corky squeaked, sounding wounded.

"So we finally meet," another, sweeter voice said from the doorway.

Traci sucked in a sharp breath, peering around Corky and Christine to stare at Brad. He looked . . . he looked exactly like a guy who'd been stabbed through the head. She looked down at the knife sticking from her bloody chest, then back to his bloody head. What an amazing coincidence!

"You must be Corky," Brad said, holding out his

hand. "I'm Brad. With the Jeep." But he was smiling, even as he locked his green-eyed gaze on Traci's speechless expression. "Guess I should warn you," he told her. "Dad's with me. I think he wants to make peace with your mom—and *I* want to talk to you about *us*. I think your phone's out of order or something."

He knew her phone wasn't out of order, and he knew she didn't want to talk to him, but something told Traci he wasn't going to take no for an answer this time.

Corky kept his arms around both girls, ignoring Brad's outstretched hand. "She doesn't want to talk to you," he began, growling like an irate puppy. "So get lost."

"If I have to go *through* you to get to her, I will," Brad countered with a smile that didn't quite reach his eyes. "I don't think it would be that hard to do, would it . . . Corky?"

"Oh . . . my . . . God," Christine cried in a squeaky whisper. "Corky's parents are here!"

With a startled cry of surprise, Corky quickly disappeared. His costume fluttered to the floor between Traci and Christine.

Traci glanced hastily around, thankful that nobody seemed to notice her friend's disappearing act. She looked at the open doorway, puzzled to find it empty.

Then she realized what Christine had done. "You

didn't," she said.

Christine looked smug. "Yep, I did. As if I didn't owe him a few. He's not the only one who can run inter- ference. Here"—she pushed Traci into Brad—"take her and go somewhere private. Try the spiderweb. It's at the end of the hall."

Before Traci could muster a protest, she found herself enfolded in her mother's artful giant-sized spiderweb. A huge black spider dangled above her head, and Brad stood blocking her exit. How could anyone look breathtaking with a fake knife stuck to his skull? But he could and he did.

She had missed him. Missed his green, green eyes and the way he stared at her as if he couldn't get enough, as if she were truly beautiful. Missed the way he made her feel warm and silly inside. Missed the way he tipped her chin or put his arm around her or held her hand, no matter who was watching or where they were.

As if he'd read her mind, he reached out and tipped her chin, his fingers lingering. "I'm flunking trig," he said.

Traci blinked. She had a strand of web caught in her eyelash, and another strand tickling her nose. What did trigonometry have to do with the fact that he'd broken her heart? Mutely, she waited for him to explain.

He gently tugged the web from her eyelash. "She's

tutoring me for extra credit. Her name's Caitlin and she's a freshman in *college*."

Surprisingly, she found her voice. "Corky said she was blond and beautiful."

"Yeah, she is," Brad admitted. "But so are you, and *you're* my girlfriend."

She swallowed hard. She wanted so very badly to believe him. "He said you two were sitting close together."

"She was writing an equation on my napkin. She had a late class and hadn't had time to eat before she drove over from Coolidge City."

Her lips were bone dry. So was her mouth, she discovered when she tried to wet her lips. "I'm supposed to believe you, just like that?"

"Yes." Brad's expression was completely serious. "Because I'm telling the truth. Dad knows about her, if you want to ask him."

But Traci could tell that he really, really wanted her to believe *him*, and him alone. Without trust, they wouldn't have much of a relationship, she knew. "Why didn't you tell me about her?"

Brad flushed. "Because I didn't want you to know how bad I stink at trig. It's embarrassing."

Traci gave him a wobbly smile. "If it makes you feel better, I stink at math altogether. English is my best subject."

"Science is mine."

"I'm sorry."

"Me, too."

She reached out and fiddled with the rip in his blood-soaked T-shirt, feeling foolish and immature and sappy-happy all in one confusing package. "Corky didn't mean any harm."

For a second Brad's jaw hardened. Then he relaxed, grinning wryly. "I know. He was just trying to protect you. I just wish he'd hung around long enough to get his facts straight, you know?"

"I know."

He held up his index finger. "See that callus? That's from dialing your number a hundred times."

"Twenty-seven," Traci said. She brought his finger to her lips and kissed the imaginary callus. "Better?"

"No. This is better."

And he kissed her, his lips warm and firm just as she remembered. Traci felt her knees grow wobbly, and had to hang on to his shoulders. He kissed her forever, or what felt like forever, before he finally pulled back long enough to whisper, "Dad's decided to cut his losses."

Traci's eyes flew open. "He's saying that it was his fault?"

Brad shrugged. "He says he needs a new car anyway."

She had news of her own. "Turns out that Corky's dad was an undercover agent." She giggled at his wowed expression. "Corky's decided to forgive him, and Mr. and Mrs. Evans are putting their house up for sale and moving away."

"So what happens to Corky now?"

Traci's smile slipped. She felt a weird sadness creep over her. Sure, Corky was mischievous and sometimes a downright nuisance, but he was still her friend. "I don't know. I guess he goes back to wherever . . . he was."

"I'd be lying if I said I'll miss him, but I know that *you* will." He pulled her close and hugged her tight, bending the rubber knife between them. "Can I ask you something?"

Thinking she'd like to stay snuggled into his chest for at least an hour or two, Traci let out a contented sigh. "Go for it."

"Is your mother the hunchback, or Frankenstein?"

"Neither. She's the one in the baby-doll pajamas, freckles, and pigtails."

"What's she supposed to be?"

"Ten years old."

They laughed together. Then their eyes met, followed by their lips. Traci felt something crawling in her hair, then along her shoulder. She knew it was the spider, and she suspected Corky was behind the prank.

But this time she didn't care.